GOOD LUCK
MISTER CAIN

GOOD LUCK
MISTER CAIN

Brian Freeborn

Secker & Warburg
London

First published in England 1976 by
Martin Secker & Warburg Limited
14 Carlisle Street, London W1V 6NN

Copyright © Brian Freeborn 1976

SBN: 436 41135 0

Printed in Great Britain by
Willmer Brothers Limited, Birkenhead

For Clo
with my love –
sorry about those walks

One

Warren Street in the summer is like a Persian market only the sun warms up cars instead of carpets. You name it they've got it, from a Maserati to a Mini, the only rule being it won't be new. The houses and shops in the side streets have all been converted into showrooms, row after row of sliding glass doors spilling motors on the pavements chrome to chrome and nose to tail scattered like they slipped off a pile behind the shopfronts. And mid-morning dealers and punters everywhere, in them on them under them, all looking for cash and a quick deal, arguing over the farts of secondhand engines. Now anyone blowing a bundle in that manor must straightaway be reckoned due for head surgery. Your average punter drops into this lot like a mouse in a snake-pit, sees the motors and probably thinks it's just another market flogging bits of iron instead of turnips, the sort of place where you do a quick barter and have it away in a nice shiny car. Although he might drive out chortling it's only a matter of time before the truth blows holes in the bonnet. They'll flog you anything you're fool enough to buy, usually something worked over with a bit of hessian and aluminium paint, and your punter fast discovers it's no good complaining. Money never comes back out of Warren Street.

It was a couple of years since I'd been there and I was feeling out of touch. Things had changed. Only small things – a shop here, a sign there – but enough to make it unfamiliar. Still, Crab and the Major had spent the best part of three days scanning the manor so we weren't taking a flier. What you've got to remember is that dealers never work alone, they can't afford to. In a cash business like that if you miss five minutes you miss the sale. Sometimes it's

1

a partnership of three but more often just two. That way they work the hard-soft routine on the punters and there's always someone minding the shop. But for us the best time is mid-day when the typists and greasers are off for their dinners and the punters swop theirs for a car. At most you've got forty-five minutes.

We'd picked a place that followed a routine. It was run by two blokes; the older one looked like an ex-commando who carried his hands about like a pair of howitzers he was trying to ignore. When he wasn't using them they got in the way and they were too big to fit into his pockets so most of the time they flapped round his knees like a pair of plaice on a string round his neck. Every so often he bunched them into fists and that made you realize how useful he must've been in the commandos. He was the hard one. The other bloke was about half his partner's size and always wore a hat. He had a nasty habit of chewing matchsticks and spitting the pulp on the showroom floor. He held up his trousers with a belt, and the waist-band, gathered into folds, drooped like tulip petals. Anyway, their typist went off with the greaser every day at one o'clock. Crab had his own thoughts about that but whatever the state of their private lives you could lay a bet they wouldn't show till two. Then the commando would be off for half an hour followed by Match-pulp at two-thirty.

We stood round the corner soaking up the sun about fifty yards from the showroom outside a tobacconist, waiting for the Major. Crab is a little bloke with a delicate skin so when I say we were soaking up the sun I mean I was, while Crab sweated under the tobacconist's awning. Crab drove a taxi when he wasn't scoring in a more intelligent fashion and if he put as much effort into regular fiddles as he put into conning his fares he wouldn't have needed a taxi at all. But he certainly kept up appearances, at least, that part of him on show to his passengers. Years of driving had made him forget he owned legs and feet. He dyed his hair black and greased it straight back off his forehead like patent leather. His moustache was pencilled at the ends where the hairs faded, like a Hollywood bandleader, and his cheeks were marked because every morning he opened his razor and forgot how delicate he was. And at a time like this Crab dangled on his nerve-ends.

At one o'clock the greaser and the typist stepped into the sun together like Crab said they would and no more than five minutes after came

2

this punter with the Major in a two-tone Herald, very slow, eyeing the shopfronts where the Major was pointing. The punter was a young bloke – young enough to believe the Major anyway – and we'd marked him outside American Express among the usual colonial mob swopping their goods for enough readies to get them home quick. The Major must've spent a bundle on the kid since opening time but the Herald was sure to pull the best part of five hundred so you had to see the outlay as an investment. The car nosed round the corner and I raised my paper to let the Major know the typist was off. The Herald stopped and I watched the Major chatting up the punter as if he was his dad, giving him the benefit of years in the motor trade he hadn't had. Crab threw me a last sick look while I grinned to make him feel better; he sighed, straightened his tie and doddled off in his crisp pin-stripe to have a natter with the commando, who at that moment was measuring the diameter of a wheel with his left. The commando straightened, a good foot taller than Crab, then with Crab leading the way they left to take a gander at the 1100 we'd parked in Fitzroy Square. The Major climbed out of the Herald just then and let the boy go. He even raised his bowler before prodding a path into Tottenham Court Road with his brolly. I watched our lad stop outside the showroom. If he made a sale we all scored.

In a while the kid and the bloke with the matchstick in his teeth came out and started poking at the Herald. The dealer lifted the bonnet, had a tinker, kicked the tyres and did a bit of revving. You could almost hear him saying what a load of rubbish. Then they got in and drove off for a test. While they were gone the sweat started stickying my palms like it always did before the whistle and I found myself counting slow and nervous till they got back, the kid's face questioning while the dealer backed the Herald against the kerb between an old Jag and a Fiat. They got out talking, then wandered into the showroom. I wiped my hands and paced the pavement looking at the briars and the Dunhills. The boy came out stuffing his wallet into his jacket and walked past the Herald like he'd never seen it. I let go my breath and scanned some more Panatellas.

The Major strode up from the opposite direction and I hoped to Christ Crab had been calm enough to recognize him on the way round the square. He stopped by the showroom and started stroking the old Jag, inspecting the paintwork, opening the doors and all that till the dealer sniffed a sale and came out to pepper him with patter. They had a bit of a chat then the Major got behind the wheel with

3

the dealer beside him and they edged out, turned right and coasted past me. If there was one trick the Major could spin out longer than a natter it was a spot of footwork on somebody else's accelerator.

I shot my cuffs, checked my watch and skipped down the tarmac. The Herald was where they'd left it and the showroom itself was cool and choked by motors on the shiny floor. The office was at the back, a wooden framework with windows. Pretending to scan the cars I edged to the office door. Racks of files and spares round the walls hanging over two desks. The Herald keys and log-book were lying on a blotter among some empty cartons. I scooped them up and was leaning on the Herald looking impatient as the commando rounded the corner. His tie was loose and the hair on his chest poked through between the buttons of his shirt, but he didn't look particularly sour after wasting his time on Crab. He was surely used to it.

'Afternoon.' He was sweating round his hairline. I patted the Herald. 'What's it worth?'

He ambled round the back and leaned the heels of his hands on the bumper. The Herald took a while getting straight.

'Bounce all gone, John?' I shrugged and stepped aside while he opened the door. 'Keys.'

I dropped them in his palm. He adjusted the seat and clambered in, knees ready to black his eyes. He started up and jockeyed the Herald to four thousand revs in short jabs.

'Got a hole in your exhaust, then?' He looked crafty. 'Right little blower, isn't she?'

'They all sound that way,' I leaned on the car, 'it's the way they're made, man.' I was being very cool.

'Sure.' He slammed the door. 'Let's have a ride.'

I got into the car and the commando crunched into first as if he could have shifted the ratio with his bare hands. The tyres yelped as we spun off the pavement; some people have no respect for other people's property. We toured the block a couple or three times, the commando cursing the clutch and everything else that moved and finally lurched back where we'd started. He switched off. 'Three hundred.'

I snorted. 'You must be joking.'

'Three hundred and that's more than you'll get anywhere else.' His eyes were steady and nasty, like he was planning another raid on Dieppe.

'Look,' I opened the door, 'I've already been offered four in Camberwell.'

4

He patted my shoulder and nearly broke my collar bone. 'If I was you John I'd take it.' He started to unwrap himself.

'So what's the matter with it, eh?'

'Nothing. It's just a bloody wreck, that's all.'

I sneered. 'Come off it. This little bird's in bloody good nick and you know it. For its age, anyway.' He started to climb out. 'Listen John. I'm a busy bloke, right? I haven't got time to rabbit to strangers. Now get this load of junk off the street and down the breakers where it belongs.'

'Three-fifty.' I checked my watch.

The Herald rocked as he slammed the door. 'You don't want a dealer. You want a bloody head-doctor.' He turned towards the show-room doors.

'Cash?' I asked.

He stopped. 'Cash.'

I looked up the street. 'OK.'

He pulled a roll from his hip pocket and counted them off in twenties. If he hadn't been so big I might have tried a snatch.

'Log-book.' He spread a hand like a plate and I gave it to him. He slapped the wad into my hand.

I tried to walk out slow. Fifty yards down the road the Major passed me in the Jag, grinding the gears like hell and looking very pissed off. It didn't look like a sale to me.

Twenty minutes later we met in The Coachman down Charing Cross Road. Crab's hair was coming unslicked and he was showing his age.

'My life.' He mopped his head. 'With success like this who needs failures?'

'Stuff it.' I flopped into a seat. 'Who takes the bloody risks?'

Crab shook his head. 'I didn't mean it like that, Harry, you know me. Don't think I don't appreciate it, I do. It's just I can't take the strain.'

'Right on, Superman. You want the bread but not the aggro, right?' I was still narked by missing a bigger score.

Crab leaned across. 'Harry. Don't take on. I like working with you. You're the best in the business.' He sighed. 'I'm getting too old.'

'You want to stick to taxis.'

The Major set down a handful of glasses. 'How much, Harry?'

I looked at them both in turn. 'Three.'

Crab jangled like a bag of glass. 'Is it worth it, I ask you?'

I stabbed a finger at his face. 'Now leave off. If either of you reckon to do better you better bloody try.'

The Major fitted a black fag into his holder. 'Three hundred? It hardly seems worth the effort.' He lit up and scanned the smoke-clouds.

I felt the blood colouring my face. 'Now look . . .'

The Major raised a hand. 'That was not intended as a criticism of you, old man. Both Crab and I respect your judgement without reservation.' Crab nodded and the Major went on. 'I merely intended to suggest that we might reconsider our scope.'

'For instance?'

The Major shrugged. 'I'm told the sale of cocaine furnishes a good return.' He flicked a speck off his lapel.

Crab wailed. 'I'm not having nothing to do with any junk. Not me.'

'Belt up.'

He gripped my arm. 'Harry for Chrissake, there's a lotta bird involved with junk. You can get sent down for ten bloody years.'

The Major stroked his upper lip. 'The higher the risk the higher the reward. Ask any banker.'

I was feeling bushed. 'Have a think about it.'

We had a quiet divi in the corner away from the mob and told each other better luck next time. I looked at the hundred in my hand. 'You know what it is, don't you?'

Crab looked up. 'What?'

'It's this bloody country boy. Private enterprise is dead. There's just no scope for brains any more.'

'Not even in coke,' Crab said to the Major.

I stuffed the hundred into my pocket. 'I dunno about you two but I need to stretch my wings. I need to be somewhere I can really score. America is where it's at, know what I mean?'

The Major knocked back his scotch and stood up. 'Sleep on it, Harry. Are you joining us on Friday?'

'I've got nothing better to do.'

The Major perched his bowler on his head. 'I shall see you at Angel's. Let's talk about it then.'

He walked out, a whole head taller than anybody else in the pub. I turned to Crab. 'You know the trouble with you? You got no spirit. No imagination. You'll never lift the loot, not the big stuff.'

'So bawl in your beer for me.' Crab went pink round the ears. 'At least I won't end up doing life.' He brightened as I drained my glass. 'Still. Maybe I'll turn a trick or three down at Angel's Friday.' He used to be good at cards.

'You can always hope.' I stood up. 'Don't take any funny money, Supersharp.'

The sun hit me like a wall outside.

Two

Back in the sixties you could be sure of nudging elbows with the famous in Scotch's. Of course that was in the days when Charlie Richardson and the Kray twins had split London down the middle and looked after their own like war-lords. Scotch's had been in Kray country and for a couple or three years it was like belonging to the biggest family in London. Georgie Farmer, Bert Roundtree, Solly O'Higgins and a hundred others would be in there night after night regular as dad's dick, knocking it back and having a rabbit. You could find anyone you wanted, every villain, pimp, layabout or brass who'd ever said boo to a bogey sooner or later passed through on his way to somewhere. Friday night used to be special because that was the night Reg or Ron used to look in. The place would be chocker, most of them there just for a goggle, and there would be old Ron, jar of Brown in his fist sprawled in his usual chair facing the door peering through the murk at the crowd. Every one of them would be wanting a word, offering something or just too scared to be anywhere else, all calling him Colonel and generally trying to get noticed or not depending on the way he scanned them. And through it all old Scotch would drift round the customers keeping things quiet, signalling the bar for refills and generally keeping himself to himself. Nobody ever said why he was called Scotch because as far as I knew the furthest north he'd been was Tottenham and he hadn't thought much of that. But he got on well with everyone, did Scotch, maybe because he'd been the only heavyweight apart from Marciano to put Cockell on his arse – and looked it – but most of all because he kept his busted nose out of other people's business. I know for a fact

8

both Reg and Ron liked him and he must've been one of the few in those days they didn't finger for as much as half a quid. He wasn't even asked.

But best of all we never had bother from the Law. In all the time I hung about Scotch's as a kid I never saw a visit from a copper who wasn't there for the friendliest reasons.

Of course times change. Scotch's is still in Dean Street all draped with red velvet and little gold tassels, stylish as ever, and Scotch still circulates through the crowd, but I'm pushing thirty-four and Reg, the Colonel, all the others, mostly gone. Straight up – you get more bother dodging Irish bombs these days than you ever got from all the old firms put together. Anyway, after the Krays left there was a bit of bad-mouthing even from blokes who'd done well out of them but I didn't join in. For one thing even Parkhurst opens its gates now and then and for another whatever they say about the Krays they did me no harm. But then if I was asked I'd say I stay out of trouble by keeping my head down and my mouth shut. Confucius he say tongue that quick end in nick and there's no porridge on my record to prove him wrong.

Anyway, the night after the Warren Street score I was on my way to the Eiger just off Frith Street to meet this scribe who'd done a little job for me. It being a warm summer's night I'd left Fulham early thinking to take the Studebaker for a pose down the King's Road and – who knows? – pick up a little something to go with my new Slumberland mattress, but the bloody traffic was like flies round a bullock's bum so I quit and drove on up to Wardour Street. The Studebaker pulls a lot of birds because after all it isn't every Wednesday you run into a 1942 saloon converted into a soft-top, which is the main reason I've got it. I'm told it's something of a collector's piece these days but since it reminds me of the best twenty minutes I ever spent in a card school it's not for sale. Of course there's more to it than you'd notice at first. It must've cost six months' pickings getting it souped up, and from the hood to the Firestones there's barely a bit of it that rolled off the line in 1942. Not that you can tell.

I left the Stud in Wardour Street and with plenty of time to kill I thought I'd call in at Scotch's and pick up the latest word. It was still light outside but walking down to the basement was like drowning in the juice from a pint of warm Guinness. It took a while to see in the dark and start wishing Scotch would do something about the ventilation. The place was already quite full, the shadows all occupied

9

by shapes mumbling over the clink of glasses while Scotch lumbered about like King Kong, thumping people on the back and stopping for a word here and there. He raised a hand and limped over when he saw me.

'Harry.' He nearly bust my fingers.

I got my hand out. 'How's business?'

'Oh mussen grumble.' Craters opened in Scotch's face when he smiled. 'Drink?'

'Drop of mother's.'

'On me.' Scotch signalled the bar and marched me to a vacant shadow. 'Siddown. Nice to see you.' He winded me with a pat and lurched off. A gin and tonic was slipped in front of me and I settled down in the velvet and oak.

It must've been ten minutes before I scanned this lucozade. She was sitting alone toying with a glass and stirring the ice with her finger. As I watched she slid her finger into her mouth and drew it out so slowly I spilt my gin. This bird had style. She wore her hair black and electric like an outsized helmet and an off-the-shoulder white blouse draped over a cleft I couldn't quite see. Rings sparked as she fingered the choker at her throat and I heard her bracelet clink as she set down her glass.

She was looking at me.

'Evening Mr Grant.' It was like copping a bucket of ice water in the middle of a dream. Somebody sat in front of me blocking the view like a wall.

'Sure it's an unexpected pleasure to see you.' I focused and damn near groaned out loud. Of all the berks I could do without, this one scooped the prizes.

'Hurly.' I changed position but he shifted in his seat and got in the way.

'Now considering the altogether absurd numbers of people who pass the time of day in this stew d'you not agree it must have been divine providence led me to yourself?'

I gave him my Palance look. His suit was several sizes too big and his shirt collar hung limp round his neck like a noose. He had a smile like the keyboard of a rotting piano and eyes like a King Cobra having a turn. I tried to look over his shoulder.

'Divine providence. The moment I saw you I said to myself now a man like Mr Grant is certain to be interested in the proposition I have to offer, and what better man to offer it to?' He sucked at

10

his glass. 'Because you see it is not every day I find a man I like sufficiently to point the way to the crock at the end of the rainbow so to speak.' He leaned forward so I could smell what he'd had for his dinner. 'Mr Grant I know you will appreciate what I have to tell you.'

I sighed and gave up trying to eye the spade.

'Stop going on Hurly, you make my nose ache. Say what you want.'

I'd had more propositions from Hurly than he'd got hairs in his earholes and he'd never set one up yet that wasn't good for a stretch. Peace only came when Hurly was doing bird and that ought to have been more often than it was; failure clung to him like mud on a swede's boots.

'Well now,' Hurly hoisted his shoulders so his head swung like washing on a line. 'What would a man like yourself be saying to some easy money?'

I yawned. 'Don't tell me. We hire an artic and snatch the Albert Hall.'

'Not at all not at all. We merely have to find the right man for a certain job.'

'What job?'

'Ah now there's the point you see....'

'Look son,' I was getting irritated. 'Bread from any source of yours has either got to be funny money or so hot it boils your bloater. Now sod off, I'm busy.'

I could've sworn she was still giving me the come-on.

Hurly wiped his nose on his sleeve. 'Find the right man and we split the commission.'

'How much?' I wasn't listening.

Hurly swallowed the dregs in his glass. 'They tell me the job could be worth twenty thousand pounds.'

I glanced up quick. 'What's the percentage?'

Hurly giggled. 'As the great and inimitable GBS said, we've established what you are, we're now discussing the price.' He grabbed my arm as I got up. 'I'm offered two per cent. That's two hundred for each of us.'

'I can count. Two ton would just slip down my trouser leg. What's the job?'

Hurly showed his keyboard. 'As I've already said, all you've to do is introduce the right man to a certain party.' He unfolded a piece of grubby paper from his pocket. 'I have here the telephone number.' He looked sly. 'Now considering it's you, Mr Grant, I might be

11

prepared to forgo my percentage for a very small – '

'Stuff it.'

The spade was smiling as I walked over. Close to she was better than she'd looked from across the room. I slid myself into the booth facing her.

'Hullo darlin. And what's a chick like you doing in a dark hole like this then?'

Her cleavage pouted when she shrugged. 'Hoping Whitey don't see me.' She put her thumb between her lips and swished her lashes at me. 'Bacardi thank you.'

I waved at the bar. 'So what do they do on a rainy night in Barbados?'

She shrugged those lovely boobs. 'Trinidad. And it doesn't rain, man.'

'Go on.' I raised my glass. 'What do they call you in the daylight?'

She smiled. 'Bitch mostly. But you can call me Kara.'

'Kara,' I told her, 'I feel a great spiritual awareness coming on.'

She widened her eyes. 'Yeah? Is that what my mammy warned me about?' The drinks arrived.

I shook my head. 'Nothing like that darlin. Just a sense of eternity generated by the accord of two human souls.'

She sipped her Bacardi. 'Eternity? Now with a nice piece of white man like you that might be easy to live through.'

'Oh I make it easy all right. You just follow me.'

'Tell me Honey,' she leaned forward, arms folded on the table. 'Is it true what they say about white men?'

'What, sweetheart?'

She traced circles with her finger on the table-top.

'You know . . .'

'No.'

'Well, back in Trinidad they always used to say . . .'

'Ah, that. I would say it depends upon the white man.'

'What about you, Honey?'

I touched her hand. It was gold and soft and caused my brain to start on the second reel of a very private film-show. She didn't take her hand away but started to stroke my wrist with one of those long forefingers.

'Maybe you ought to find out,' I breathed.

She grinned pert and pretty. 'Maybe.'

I withdrew my wrist because I couldn't stand it. 'Right. Now there's no need for a girl like you to sit around here all night, is there?'

She stroked her choker. 'And you know a better place, is that right Honey?'

'Right, love, I do.' I swallowed. 'Now if you had no other arrangements for tonight I'd suggest a nice quiet evening somewhere that suits you. Something to eat, then . . .'

Her hand was reaching out for mine again. 'Then what, Sweetheart?' I could feel my pulse knocking like it wanted out.

'Depends.'

She watched me over the rim of her glass and her eyes were wicked. 'I like that best. Depends.'

I drained my glass. 'Come on then.'

She shook her head. 'Can't, Honey.'

'Oh leave off, gel. Come on.'

Something told me I'd already missed the mark. Worse. My hands had started to sweat.

'I gotta meet a friend,' she was still smiling.

'Fine.' I started to get up.

'Hi Honey.' She was looking behind me.

Even as I turned I was cussing myself. My number one rule and the first bit of tease in sight made me forget it like it never existed. I glanced over my shoulder. From where I crouched they looked like two of the biggest spades I'd ever seen and I thought Christ if ever I shake loose I'll make donations to police charity for the rest of my life so help me. They must've added up to fourteen feet between the two of them and the nearest one had his hand on my shoulder. The hand was manicured, the fingers were ringed with sparklers and the cuffs were crisp and white.

'You talking, boy?'

The one behind wore a white linen suit and a moustache that drooped to his chin.

'Me?' I laughed. 'I never talk to strange men.'

'But sweetheart,' the bird was all petulant. 'I thought we were going out.' She giggled into her Bacardi. The nearest spade gripped me under the arm and beckoned me upright. I didn't have much choice. Standing up they were taller than ever and as they pressed in close I caught a sniff of expensive after-shave. Neither of them looked any better for it though. The one nearest me wore shades that

13

wrapped round his face and his head was shaved, tight black skin stretched over bone.

'Where were you going, feller?' His teeth shone.

I eased out of his grip and straightened my jacket. 'This suit cost a lotta bread.'

The second spade jerked a thumb at the one who'd been handling me. 'This here's Jesus Largo.' He pointed at Kara. 'That's his woman. You got yourself plenty shit, man.'

I tried to turn sideways. 'Him too, come Easter. Nice girl.' I could hear the girl in question titter behind me.

'Like my friend says,' Largo turned his blind face to mine, 'You in shit, White-eyes.'

Kara panted. 'Show him, Largo. He asked me to do it with him.' Largo didn't seem to move his mouth when he spoke.

'Nobody messes with Jesus Largo's property.'

At times like this I thought the Seventh Cavalry would come in very handy. Or even just one horse. I cleared my throat. 'You're new here, Jesus, right? Look, I gotta lot of friends. I got friends you wouldn't even see coming, know what I mean?' Scotch was moving over from the far side. 'Now if I was you Jesus I'd just drop the whole thing and have a drink.'

Scotch wasn't exactly the Seventh Cavalry but I've never been so glad to see him. He laid a paw on Largo's shoulder.

'Help you gennlemen?'

His hand stayed where it was and I knew how heavy it was. Largo might've been scanning Scotch through his shades but you couldn't tell. There was a long pause. Suddenly he showed his teeth and very gently removed Scotch's hand.

'Get me a coke.' The spades sat down like I was the Invisible Man.

'See you, Honey.' Kara was grinning like some crazy voodoo doll.

'Bitch,' I mouthed, and moved off behind Scotch.

'Alright Harry?' Scotch didn't like his place disturbed.

I nodded. 'Ta. Keep an eye on those buggers.'

Scotch winked and I made for the stairs. 'Tra, Jesus. Watch the thorns.'

They didn't look up.

Three

The Eiger is one of those boozers they had to put into fancy dress to catch the customers. It's full of wood, not wood soaked with nicotine and varnish as you'd expect, but wood that's been carved and sanded and scrubbed till it comes across dead as a pavement on Sunday. All this in the name of convincing the swedes that the Alps start on the west side of Charing Cross Road. This white wood makes the place very light, not at all like a boozer, so light cheery and safe it makes you want to throw up. And being a safe boozer they get, apart from the swedes, straight customers. Well. Straight by the Law's standards anyway. You get more birds in there too but mostly arty types in advertising or something, all jeans, cheesecloth and straight blonde hair round sunglasses. The blokes with them are usually carrying cans of film, wearing roll-neck sweaters, and calling each other Dominic and Nigel. And I was there because the scribe I was meeting had twisted my arm.

Alfred Mehrstein was sitting in a corner underneath his black Homberg and belted raincoat. He never wore anything else summer or winter, blinking out through steel-rimmed specs with eyes that faded more each time.

'Evening Alfred.'

He peered through his specs. 'Good evening Harry. You are late.'

'Don't give me aggro, Grandad. I've just settled two so you won't cause me bother. What're you drinking?'

'Cognac, thank you.'

I got a drop of mother's for myself and settled down next to him. He was rolling a cigarette. Alfred's cigarettes were about as thick as

15

a blade of desert grass and once in his mouth they stayed till they shrank under his moustache, which was yellowed like a wad of charred paper. Ash spilled like snow over his raincoat when he reached for his drink.

'Your liver must look like a well-done hamburger,' I told him.

Alfred shrugged and spread his hands. 'At my age there are few pleasures left.' He nodded to himself. 'Good cognac is one of them.'

'Prosit.' I took a mouthful of gin. 'How's business?'

He polished his specs, showing eyes reddened from years over a drawing-board. 'Not bad. Not good. Nothing like the old days, Harry.'

'Nothing ever is.'

Wisps of white hair floated out under his hat-brim. 'In the old days I should have made a fortune. A fortune. Now is too late.'

'Never mind. Wait till they start issuing ration books again. Can't be long now.'

He sighed. 'Ah, ration books. It was so easy in those days.' His old eyes watered memories. 'Did I tell you I had a staff in those days? In Vienna three people were working for me. Twenty books a week, and, I don't know, five or six identity cards as well.' He shook his head. 'Prosperity destroys people like you and me, Harry. Prosperity destroys demand.'

I choked on my Gilbey's 'Prosperity? Here? Leave off.'

That seemed to tickle him. He patted my arm. 'You are a good boy, Harry.'

I nudged him. 'Got my parcel?'

He pushed his fingers into his raincoat pocket and wrestled out a brown envelope. Panting, he tossed it into my lap.

'All there?'

'All there.' His ash splashed into his glass. 'Letters of introduction, references, driving licences, passports, all there.' He tried to fish out his ash as I squinted into the envelope. I needn't have. We'd worked together a good few years. I pulled out a white envelope from my inside pocket.

'Cop this. It's that heavy it's ruining my new gear.'

Alfred was awake again. 'One-hundred-fifty?'

I nodded. 'Like we said.'

He slipped the envelope into his raincoat without checking. 'From next time we make it for one hundred pounds a time.'

'A hundred? You old sod.'

'Ach Harry, we have all to make a living. And everything is going

16

up, all the time inflation, inflation. How does a man feed himself otherwise?'

'You're a villain,' I told him.

He beamed. 'I know. And so are you.'

'That's different. If there's one thing I can't abide it's a Kraut crook.'

'I am Austrian.'

'Same thing. Bloody foreigner.'

'I am Austrian and I have lived here longer than have you.'

I sucked a slice of gin-soaked lemon. 'Not the same. I've got centuries of proper English blood in me. Centuries.'

He was trying to dust the ash off his raincoat. 'Yes, that would explain your criminal mind.'

I had to laugh. 'Like you said we all gotta make a living. OK. A hundred quid a time. But don't blame me if I can't raise the customers.'

He winked. 'They will pay.'

Over the noise of the mob I heard a laugh I thought I recognized. She was standing against the bar drinking a Campari soda, easily the most noticeable bird there. There was something about Dina that drew immediate attention, which was just as well since she spent ten hours a day stripping on the circuit and a stripper that can't draw her audience might as well wrap her costume in her hanky and go digging spuds. She was a big girl and lovely with it. Her scarlet skirt swirled round the top of her boots as she gestured and from the expression on the face of the bloke she was rabbitting at I could tell she was making another kill. He was straight out of the studio, roll-neck sweater and all, sweating with the effort of keeping up. Dina had on one of those high-collared white blouses which end in a puff of lace at the wrist and every time she moved her blouse looked fit to bust its buttons. This bloke was having a hard time of it. Dina was with another bird, a mate from the circuit probably, and they were both going hammer and tongs at roll-neck who didn't know what to grin with next. I spoke to Alfred.

'Let's put some life in your old veins.' I yelled across the boozer and Dina stopped in mid-sentence and cast about, blouse rippling. She saw me, waved both arms and shrieked before swallowing her Campari and swaying across the floor. The air was suddenly heavy with scent.

'Harry!' She chucked both arms round my neck and kissed me on the mouth which was nice.

17

I grinned. 'How you been?'

'Great.' She stroked my knee. 'But better for seeing you.'

'Dina, this is Alfred.'

Alfred looked like he might try and hoist himself out of his chair but Dina was a warm-hearted girl. She reached across and nuzzled his moustache. 'Hullo Alfred.' She turned to me. 'Are all your friends as nice?'

Alfred liked getting nuzzled and he liked to be told he was nice. His cheeks flushed.

'No,' I said, 'only Alfred.'

'Correct, yes.' Alfred's grin was splitting his face. I went and got another round and found the two of them nattering like life-long buddies when I got back.

'Your friend has been married three times,' said Dina.

'Go on.' He hadn't told me.

'Six children.' Alfred stroked his moustache.

Dina raised hands and eyebrows together. 'I might've known from the look of him.'

'How's the circuit treating you, then?' I asked.

Dina had good strong teeth. 'I take the bumps with the grinds.' She bundled her skirt up over her knees, showing a good length of fish-net.

'On duty?'

She tugged at the tops of her boots, watching me scan her legs. 'Not tonight. Day of rest.' She breezed scent over me. 'Night off, Harry Grant. Anything could happen and probably will.' She twisted a strand of hair and threw the look she used on the punters in the front row.

'What about your mates?' I nodded at Roll-neck and the other bird.

'Huh? Oh, that's Georgie.'

'Why do we not ask him for a drink?' Alfred must've been feeling spry. Dina giggled and patted his cheek.

'Georgie's with me on the circuit. She's due at the Nell Gwynne in ten minutes.'

'Not her night off.' Alfred nodded wisely.

Dina winked. 'Don't be greedy, dear.'

Georgie downed her Campari, grinned at Roll-neck and skipped over carrying her little case. She was a handsome little mystery, slighter than Dina.

18

'Cheers my love,' she blew a kiss. 'See you in your tassels.'

'Mind how you go,' called Dina. 'Kick their balls if they grope.'

Georgie wiggled out the door.

Alfred was struggling to his feet. 'Ah well. . . .'

Dina looked disappointed. 'Where you going?'

When Alfred stood he wasn't much taller than Dina sitting down. He fumbled with the lid of a pocket watch.

'Home.' He raised his hat. 'I have very much enjoyed our talk.'

' 'S long lovie,' Dina planted a kiss under the brim of his hat. 'See you some more.'

'I hope so, yes. Goodbye Harry. Call me.'

Alfred wrestled a path to the street.

'All right Mr Grant,' Dina held my hand in hers. 'Night off. What's on the menu?'

'What d'you fancy?'

She licked her lips. 'Something . . . succulent.'

'Funny you should say that.'

Roll-neck was standing beside me glass in hand, grinning stupidly. His suit was very neat and his hair was styled so careful he would have burst into tears if somebody messed it. He was wearing black patent-leather boots. 'Good evening.' He was wary.

Dina was everybody's mate. 'This is Simon.'

Simon jabbed a hand at me like his arm was a piston-rod and sat next to Dina. 'If you're ready, Dina, I thought we might have a bite somewhere.'

Dina giggled. 'Not now thanks.'

Simon flushed. 'When?'

'Dunno dear.' She shook his hand. 'Another time maybe, OK?'

'As you wish.' Simon stood double dignified. 'Perhaps I shall see you again.'

'I hope so.' Her smile could've melted armour plate. Simon left his drink.

'Who the hell was that?' I watched him go.

'Dunno. You know me.' She stroked back her hair. 'Some straight looking for a bit of rough I suppose. It gives me a lift now and then.' She grinned. 'Let's start the hors d'oeuvres.'

Frith Street was frozen with cars in a neon blaze. The crowds shuffled along the pavements, swedes gaping at sex-shops and strip joints, Maltese rabbiting on the sidewalks, trendies lugging bottles of wine and the occasional local noticeable by the way he sliced through the mob. We walked arm in arm across Wardour Street and up into Berwick Street where it was calmer. Dina's gaff was over a chemist's and the gloom of the hall and stairs didn't leave you ready for the lushness of her place. Everything was white. I waded through the pile on the carpet and settled into a white leather couch. Dina drew the curtains and turned up the standard lamp which stood on a curly wooden stand. She poured a couple of drinks and sat close on the couch. 'Glad I ran into you, Harry.'

I kissed her on the nose. 'Some people are born lucky.'

She nuzzled my ear and ran her lips down the line of my jaw while her fingers unbuttoned my shirt. 'My,' she whispered, 'it's warm in there.' I lifted her chin and kissed her long and slow. 'Like music, Harry?'

'Sure.'

She was made for watching. She swayed to the record player, selected a disc and turned to face me, stroking her hips. 'I enjoy my work, you know?'

I was glad about that. The rhythm picked up while she unbuttoned her blouse, starting at the throat and working down pearl by pearl to her waist. She drew the blouse out of her skirt, let it float to the carpet and reached for the zip at her waist. I waited till she stood nude but for the chain round her belly. She was firm and hot against me as we sank into the pile. 'Harry you bastard.' She put her tongue in my ear. 'Where have you been?'

Four

I came to with a jump about seven and had a spot of bother sorting out where I was. My lungs hurt. They hurt because Dina had planted her head on my rib-cage, hair spreading down my belly like a gold cape. There were traces of lipstick on my chest and my shoulders stung with the tram-lines she'd carved with her nails. I scanned the room, head clearing. It was all drapes and fancy satins with a carpet like the living-room and she was the only bird I ever met that sported a canopy like a parachute over the bed. I eased out, shoving a pillow under her head. She stirred and curled like a baby, hair now spilling over the sheets. I stood blinking in the middle of the room wondering where I'd put my gear. The bedroom door was wide, forgotten in the rush, and I saw my best trousers crumpled round the lamp-stand like a dosser left out to dry. I swore and shook them out. Pants, shirt, jacket and tie were stashed in various nooks and I collected them on the way to the bathroom. The bathroom was littered with bottles of this and that, tops lying about, stuff you rub under your arms, up your nose and down your legs, pink stuff and white stuff, Dina had the lot; she could've used a few more cupboards to cope with the load. I bust a jar of face-cream looking through the shelves but being a kindly girl Dina was not one to inconvenience her friends by sending them home unshaven. Behind the clutter was a brush and razor with a tube of Ingrams. The water was steaming and I felt better when I'd finished. I took a cold shower and stepped out bristling like a porcupine.

I sat among the gadgets in the kitchen putting on shirt socks and shoes between bites of bread and jam and sips of Nescafé. Then

I washed up. I do not enjoy cleaning kitchens but then, as certain parties not unconnected with the Law have pointed out, my preference for polished surfaces has more than once preserved me from one of the little horrors that fate sprinkles before us on the stoney road to death. I speak of course of the nick. Tidiness has become a habit with me, which is why I hate climbing into yesterday's gear.

Judging by the display of quality around me the silver G-string lark must've been paying pretty good, so good I wouldn't have thought twice about getting out there myself if I thought there was a demand for a shape like mine, or even muscling in on the management of same, but that carried its own bother. I wouldn't have minded providing envelopes for the Law, that was a normal overhead, but I wouldn't fancy splitting percentages with the acid spring-cleaners. Unless you could raise your own mob it was a dodgey business.

At eight I was ready. I brushed down my suit and waded into the bedroom to tell my hostess goodbye but she looked too good to wake, lying there clutching the sheet to her chin leaving the rest of her rounded and displayed. I kissed my fingers and laid them on the cleft of her buttocks. She didn't stir.

Soho's a great place early in the morning. The shopkeepers are raising their shutters and chucking buckets of water over the pavement, scrubbing it down and swopping jokes. There's a smell of baking bread which takes me right back to Canning Town. All the signs are quiet and you can see just how mean they are in the daylight. Places that scream glamour during the night look like worn-out whores in the morning and the feeling's just the same – you wonder why you thought they were anything else. The Stud was parked on the same yellow line; that's one benefit of having some of the Law on the payroll – it must've been years since I got a ticket up West.

Me and the Stud coasted up Wardour Street across the traffic in Oxford Street and into Tottenham Court Road, filtering down the Euston Road and into a side turning off Eversholt Street. I parked on a meter-bay this time since I couldn't bank on being recognized that far north and there's no sense advertising yourself. I ran up the steps into the station, already milling with people that poured into the tube like water down a plughole. The musak tinkled while the fuzz busied themselves getting the last of the dossers to their feet. I bought a brown envelope at Menzies and weaved to the luggage lockers near platform one. Standing between the rows of lockers I

22

took out Alfred's envelope and removed two driving licenses which I slipped into my pocket. The rest of the papers went into the box which I locked, slipping the key into my breast pocket. Then I had a cup of stand-up tea in the Railbar while I addressed the brown envelope to myself care of Trafalgar Square Post Office. I never feel right till my second cup of something in the morning and I could feel the blood getting to my toes as I drove south again. Or maybe it was anticipation.

The trouble with this country is they don't give you a drink till half-eleven unless you're a meat porter so I left the Stud in its usual place and went and beat on Scotch's door. Scotch doesn't take chances. He took ten minutes to get there and open up just enough to scan what Herbert was busting the door in the middle of the night. 'Christ.' He looked bad, short grey hair spiking in all directions and grey eyes gummed by sleep. His vest was none too clean.

'It's the fairies come to wish you luck.'

'Wassermadder?' Scotch scratched his chest.

'Come for a quickie,' I told him as he slipped the chain, 'what you got?'

'You lost your marbles?' The place looked horrible when he switched the light on.

'Bloody hell,' I breathed, 'it's a wonder I'm not poisoned grogging in a shit-house like this.'

'You don't have to.' Scotch was waking up.

'I'll have a drop of Gilbey's,' I slapped a note on the counter. 'Why don't you get this place cleaned up?'

'Piss off.' Scotch looked as sour as his booze as he poured a double.

'Go on,' I told him, 'half a glass.'

He worked the optic like a bike pump. I took the glass and stood over the sink behind the bar, took a mouthful, chucked back my head and gargled like Johnny Weismuller. 'Keep-fit exercises.' I spat into the sink. Scotch shook his head and limped to the stairs.

'Shut the door when you go.'

In five minutes I smelled like a still.

One thing about that time of the morning is nobody is likely to get you to blow into a little bag, which was just as well in my case because I could have destroyed us all with a puff. I parked round the corner from King Edward Post Office and waited. My two customers entered the building at nine-thirty. I loosened my tie, rumpled my hair, checked Alfred's driving licences and followed them in. They were big fellers both and either one could have eaten me up a dark alley without his dentures which was why we were not up a dark alley at this particular moment.

King Edward's is like a bloody castle, all marble and gilt, echoing like Moses' bathroom. The columns stand like redwoods bursting into stone leaves as they touch the ceiling and the main floor makes you want to head for the safety of the walls like an ant. Queues were already forming at the counters and I sat down at one of the writing tops to watch my two lads. They stood against a column trying to look natural but if I'd been the Law one glance would've had me squawking for air support. They were both smoking and when I say smoking I mean they were almost eating fags, hot ash and all. They were wearing raincoats, though outside it had the makings of a hot summer's day, and one sported a trilby pulled over his eyes like Humphrey Bogart seeing off Ingrid Bergman at the airport. The other had a hairstyle like a monk only not so neat and his head was knobbly and very distasteful. I doddled over, palms prickling. 'Morning.' They surrounded me like a rugby scrum, all two of them, pressing close with dark looks.

'Got 'em?' The one with the hat was almost goosing me so I backed off into the bald one who suddenly sniffed the air. 'He's pissed.'

The Hat muscled in. Gin didn't bother him. 'Have you got them?'

I showed the licences. 'Seeing as it's you I'll let you have the both for three hundred.'

The Monk snatched the licences and flipped through. 'Where's the rest?'

I raised a finger. 'Uh-uh. First the gelt.'

They looked at each other and the Hat tried a different tack. 'Come on. You'll get your money.'

I held out my hand. 'I know.'

'Look.' The Monk could've put the frighteners on Henry Cooper just trying to look friendly. 'George and me was talking about the chances of, well, doing a deal with you.' He was inspecting my face, trying to guess how pissed I was and how slow I was like to be. 'Three hundred's a lotta gelt, you know.'

'No deals.'

I could tell they were having bother keeping their paws off me but I had something they needed first.

24

The Monk glanced over his shoulder. 'Right. Give it to him, Francis.'

For a second I thought he was telling Francis to put the boot in and so did Francis until George snapped his head impatiently. There could well have been a nasty accident.

'Give it to him. Then let's scarper.' Francis was a bit slow catching on but eventually he took out a bundle. They waited while I riffled through the tenners. 'Come on come on.' George's nervousness was starting to show. I picked the locker key out of my pocket between thumb and forefinger like the vicar taking tea.

'There you are.'

They stared blank and stupid as if they expected the key to turn into passports.

'Euston station locker fifty-nine.' I dropped the money into my envelope, licked the flap and stuck on a stamp. They looked choked, like they'd been robbed, which considering who they were was dead funny. I raised a finger.

'Cheers.'

I turned on the marble and took two steps. George was ahead of me. 'Hang about. How do we know this isn't a con?'

I pushed past. 'You don't.'

'Lay one on him George.' Like I said, Francis was not exactly genius material.

'Belt up!' George was sweating as he scanned the hall. I dodged round an old man and got him between them and me. Francis cussed and reached for my arm as I dropped the envelope into the letter-box like a centre-half scoring a goal.

'About this key.' They had me sandwiched again and George was starting to look seriously narked. 'Francis and me think you ought to accompany us to Euston, don't we, Francis?'

Francis blinked until he caught on. 'That's right, George.' He started to leer and it was clear he was working up to a spot of Harry-bashing.

I sighed. 'I'd love to, guys, but honest I can't. I gotta go to work. Why don't you two just take a cab up Euston and collect by yourselves?'

'Good idea.' Francis fingered my arm. 'You show us the way on account of we're new here.' They took an arm each.

Well it was obvious something had to be done. Breaking loose I lurched into the middle of the hall like King Kong. I kicked at the

25

air round my feet like I was getting chased by a wolf-pack, which when you think about it wasn't far short of the truth. I beat my chest, waved my arms and nearly fell backwards. Things went quiet all of a sudden. George and Francis were cowering near the letter-boxes while I tried a spot of shadow-boxing round the columns, accompanying myself with a series of Alpine yodels. That really got them rolling in the aisles. There was a flutter behind the counter, a quick consultation and somebody slipped through a door at the back. The queues were looking interested. A smartish woman sailed through the main doors done up to the nines in twin-set and pearls and a floppy hat. I galloped towards her on all fours. She dropped her handbag and did a couple of quick side-steps. I sniffed at her knees and she clutched at the hem of her skirt and shrieked good and loud as she backed against the wall. As I stuck out my tongue two coppers bust in the side door. I stood up, dusted my trousers and picked up the woman's handbag. She shook so bad she could hardly hold it. 'Good morning Madam,' I said, 'I must apologize for any inconvenience I may have caused you.' Two pairs of hands fell on my shoulders. 'Morning lads.' I turned to face the blue jaws of Old Bill himself.

Old Bill wrinkled his nose. 'Pissed as a fart.'

There was no sign of George or Francis when the Law marched me out.

26

Five

It's a nasty place, the nick, even if you are only stopping over. This was the second night I'd spent at whatsername's pleasure and things hadn't got any better. It's the smell mostly. Now I've never done bird apart from overnight visiting but there must be something about me because as soon as Old Bill claps eyes on yours truly he starts smacking his lips and reaching for the record. Then I watch the steam whistle out of his ear-holes when he can't find anything on me and from then on it's downhill because he may not know what I've done or what I'm about but he can tell I'm not just another John Pratt. What can you do with people like that? Still, when you consider the alternative back in the Post Office a drop of porridge suits me any day. So I spent the night in the nick with a couple of yobs going on about some Herbert who'd grassed. Listening to them I was glad I wasn't this particular Herbert. They were only kids with no more than forty years between the two of them.

And all night long the gates clanged, the screws' boots echoed and blokes howled murder in their sleep.

For the third morning running I put on the same clothes and joined the line of dossers and piss-artists for the daily knuckle-rap. I left the carbolic and the gunmetal eyes of the screws downstairs among the clatter of slopping-out and tried to shut out the shock of Snow Hill in the sunlight. Then me and the rest were herded in the Black Maria two abreast and driven like meat to the courts.

I waited downstairs for a bit then took my turn for a sniff of the polish on the panelling. The beak was an old boy who'd done this

27

particular dance a thousand times and was bored rigid by the music. A kid up ahead got six months for busting a shop window and the party behind him copped three for insulting the Law. That made me wonder if the price might come too high but I needn't have worried. My performance in the Post Office was described as a Nuisance to the Public brought on by an excess of alcohol and the beak hoped a day and a night inside would teach me a lesson. I pleaded ever so guilty. Twenty quid and a reprimand. I'd sooner have spent the night in the Dorchester but it would've cost more. As it was I stepped out three ton heavier than the day before.

Well, two hundred and eighty net.

It was hot outside. The trouble in the summer is you can see the muck from the cars drifting at the bottom of the street like sewage in the Grand Canyon and you realize how sick you might be without knowing it. I once saw a picture of the lungs of a bloke who'd lived in Bethnal Green for sixty years and I've been trying to hold my breath ever since. Still, the Public was poncing about in its summer gear and even the fuzz were wearing their sweat-stains like medals. The Stud was where I'd left it but being a stranger I'd copped two quid's worth of nasty on the windscreen. I stuffed it down the nearest gulley, opened the hood and turned the radio up full blast, cruising down to Fulham in an armour of pop off Radio One. I tried a vault over the door when I stopped and tore the leg of my trousers on the handle. Marge was in – I saw her through the downstairs curtain – but she drew back when I faced the window: we never talk unless the rent's late.

The house isn't actually on the main road but in one of those streets leading off the east side. Of course the west has been taken over by berks in Range Rovers and denim suits who fancy a bit of Real Life as long as it's close to Chelsea but they don't dodge the traffic. The gaff isn't bad as apartments go down the Wandsworth Bridge Road, two rooms showing Victorian decoration which I tried to lose when I moved in. I mean you can't expect a bird to be impressed by a string of plaster grapes round the cornice when you bring her back. But most of the cost went on the stereo, that and the carpet, which is rust coloured and wall-to-wall.

I dropped my suit on the couch, bundled shirt socks and pants in the wardrobe and sank into a hot bath with the radio propped on the basin and a glass of light balanced in the soap-dish. It felt very good humming along and pondering what I'd do with the three ton waiting fatly in Trafalgar Square and I still hadn't made up my mind when I left about one cutting the air with the creases in my light-weight drills. I took an easy trip along the embankment. The swedes were out on the river and the boats were listing as they scarpered side to side photographing the backs of warehouses and power-stations. Parliament Square was like Southend at Easter – except in Southend they speak English. I humped the Stud up the pavement outside Trafalgar Square Post Office and slipped through the tourists marking crosses on pictures of Nelson for the purpose of identification. It was too warm in there but I didn't have to wait long. I flipped my driving licence over the counter as proof of identity and the spade behind rummaged in a rack at the rear and came out with my brown envelope and I thought our postmen were wonderful. I scratched my name, winked at the golly and did a single-action vault into the Stud outside. I took off the pavement with a double Paramount wheel-spin and headed north.

Angel Horrocks runs a caff in Chinatown off Shaftesbury Avenue, and driving through the manor you'd swear the booze had rattled your marbles and you'd ended up in Canton. Chinese picture-houses, Chinese eating houses, even Chinese cat-houses where all you've heard about slanty eyes is true but not a word of English spoke or wrote for a good quarter-mile excepting of course Angel's. The Chinese hang about in gangs outside doorways and up alleys, little blokes with black hair looking like it belongs to somebody else all jawing away in Christ knows what, pushing junk and goosing girls. Well, in the middle of this lot Angel's was like a mission station in Outer Mongolia, which is to say you could be sure of a good game and a few jars while the natives stayed outside and didn't give you bother.

The smell in the caff was wicked and I thought what a way to make a living, especially for a man like Angel who in his day had been the best peter-man in the country. Angel's missus stood behind the counter frying chips in a blackened pan. She couldn't see what she was doing on account of having to squint through a wisp of smoke that curled up her nose from the fag in her mouth. When I called out two inches of ash fell in the chips.

'All right if I go upstairs Missus?'

She turned. 'Wait.' When she coughed the skin under her chin quivered like a turkey's. I sat between the tea-drops on one of the

29

Formica tables while she wiped the chip-grease on her overall, adjusted her yellow wig and pushed a button on one of those squawk-boxes that take the orders.

'Dad?' There was a pause because Angel did not like to be called Dad. Then a squawk. 'Harry Grant.' The box screeched. She turned to me.

'All right. You can go up.'

The room at the top of the stairs was part of Angel's gaff but it was only used for card schools and piss-ups. The curtain bulged over the open window, flashing cracks of sunlight at the edges and a fan hummed on the chest of drawers in the corner. The table in the middle was circular and draped in smoke frayed by the breeze. Angel was fat, so fat he had trouble breathing and hadn't seen the state of his feet for years, but for all that he moved amazingly quick. He was wearing a vest and a pair of grey bags held up by an old army belt. We shook hands.

'Where's the action, then?'

Angel ran a paw through the odd bits of hair he had left. 'Plenty of action here boy if you can stand the pace.'

'Stay cool Angelface. Today I'm outta your class so don't come the frighteners.'

'How much?'

'Ton and a half?'

'You're in.' Angel sucked his teeth and waved the others around the table. 'Make room for a mark.'

Crab got me a chair. 'Nice safe game if I was you, Harry. The Galloping Major's on form again.'

The Major stubbed out a fag. 'I say. Tell him he will need the balance he kept for himself in Warren Street.' Very cool. Today his hair was parted straight down the middle and all he lacked was a little silver-topped cane. But it was the fourth that put my back up. 'Got your cheque-book, Hurly?' He didn't even look up.

'Who needs cheque-books?' asked Crab, 'he's got the IRA, hasn't he?'

I stared round the table. 'But I thought Hurly was a Protestant.'

Angel scratched his chest and yawned. 'Glass of brown, Harry?' He passed over a can.

'What's the game?'

'Five-card. Straight.'

30

I scanned my watch. 'Till six?' I sipped at the foam bulging over the rim of my glass.

'Divesting you of a mere one hundred and fifty pounds should take approximately half that time.' The Major selected a fag from his case.

I spread my hands. 'So what am I waiting for?'

It wasn't a bad afternoon. Crab had been good in his time but these days his nerves were getting in the way like they did on a job. After a couple of careful hands I was reading him like a book, a twitch here and a sniff there told whether his cards were worth the stake and I couldn't help feeling a bit sorry about it, not that I actually wanted to get beaten. The Major was playing better than I'd ever seen, coming across with a quiet confidence that gave away as much as a beak on the bench, but Hurly was the wickedest. He played without speaking, just watching the rest of us, counting out his chips and leaving the dealer to count the cards he discarded, nasty little eyes flicking round the table. But for all that he wasn't doing too well and judging by the way he touched his coat pocket he was running a bit low. The rules said no credit and he knew it. By half-five I was coming out evens and if I was going to score it had to be soon. Angel dealt me a couple of fives with a mixed bag not worth the bother so I chucked the rubbish and called for three. Crab took a complete hand and threw them back, the vein in his forehead standing out scarlet. Angel and the Major took two each and Hurly gnawed his thumb-nail and tossed out one. Angel had dropped me three ladies.

'There you go.' I started with a tenner. The Major sucked his fag-holder and counted out fifteen.

'Another five.'

Hurly, eyes fixed on his cards, pushed out sixteen.

The Major winked at me. True, it is written that he that starts a hand like he's sitting on a rocket gets his arse burnt but this was ridiculous. Angel mumbled, hissed, and chucked down his cards. 'Bastards.'

This was where we geed up. 'Let's see . . .' I counted them out, 'six to see you . . .' Hurly twitched 'and another . . . ten.'

The Major frowned, drawing the point of his parting down between his eyes. 'Very well. Eleven to see you, Harry, plus . . . five.'

'Fifty, Hurly,' I said, 'do yourself a favour.'

Hurly was bright red. He counted out fifteen to see, and with a

31

look meant to warn me off, added one. I snorted. 'You playing in this game then, Hurly?'

He didn't answer. I considered my lovely ladies.

'Right. Sixteen to see you, and . . . another five.'

The Major was scanning me like he'd just twigged. His face cracked into a grin as he shook his head. 'No.' He laid his cards face down and rocked back in his chair I nodded to Hurly. 'Me and you, old son. Hope you've got the readies on you.'

Crab's chair creaked as he leaned forward. Everybody was waiting on Hurly. He counted out fifteen, then spoke for the first time. 'Raise you twenty.' You could've cut the atmosphere with a knife. I watched Hurly. If my guess was right he was down to his last few quid, he'd been holding on tight till now when he thought he'd make a clean kill by scaring off the opposition. But whatever he had in his hand he wouldn't be able to pay for if pushed hard enough. And anyway by this time I was dead curious. 'Your twenty and another . . . thirty.'

Hurly bust his cool. 'Will you lend us a tenner?' He almost shrieked at Angel.

Angel didn't raise his eyes. 'No.'

'For the love of God!'

'No.'

I was feeling double lucky and didn't know why.

'Hurly. Remember trying to flog me something down at Scotch's?' Hurly's face was the colour of sour milk. 'The phone number. Remember?'

His mouth twitched and he spoke with difficulty. 'That could be worth a lot of money.'

I slapped my cards face down. 'Do me a favour. You're short of readies, right? So take a chance with what you've got. That's what the game's about, right, Angel?'

'Right.'

The Major crossed his legs and flicked his ash on Angel's floor. 'What telephone number?'

I grinned. 'A sort of passport to paradise.'

'Eh?' said Angel.

'Could be worth a bundle, couldn't it, Hurly? Even thirty nicker. Go on. You're a dead cert to win so what difference will it make, eh?'

Hurly breathed very quick while his eyes twitched from the kitty to his cards and back again. His fingers hesitated at his jacket pocket, withdrew, then stabbed in and bounced back clutching a bit of paper. 'See you!'

I yawned. 'Full House.'

'Let's see 'em.' Hurly knocked over his chair as he jumped to his feet.

'Two fives . . .' I spread them out, 'and . . . three beauties.'

I thought Hurly would bust a vein. His face went scarlet, then purple and back to white all inside five seconds. He started to say something, choked, looked at each of us in turn, then ran for the door. The gaff shook as he pounded down the stairs. The Major wrinkled his nose. 'I have always said that fellow was a bad loser.'

I raked in the kitty and inspected Hurly's paper. The name on it was Drake and a phone number was scribbled beneath. 'Passport to paradise.' I winked at Angel, who was having a good scratch.

It was coming on six and time for Scotch's. Angel slouched off grunting about committments and Crab belted out hollering about his taxi so the Major and I cleared the table and walked on up to Dean Street telling each other how Angel wasn't what he used to be which conversation led us, like it always did, to speculate on the condition of a man's spirit after twenty years of marriage. He's always good for a natter, the Major, and we settled down in Scotch's in what you might call a philosophical mood and got down to some philosophical drinking after which I usually end up dead morbid. Too much philosophy has that effect on me. About half-seven the Major began to see how low I was getting and must've thought it was because of him, which it wasn't. He stood up a bit unsteady.

'Where you going?'

'Home.' He swayed over the table.

I caught a glass as he raised his arms .'This . . .' he stared about, 'is a young man's world. You get on and enjoy yourself.' I started to stand but he leaned on my shoulder. 'Please.' He was scratching his head like his fingers would unearth some memory. Then his face brightened.

'Ah. That telephone number.' He breathed vermouth into my face. 'What . . . what're you going to do about it, old chap?'

I flipped Hurly's paper on the table. 'You have it.'

The Major was shocked, wagging his head until a thick grey curl shook loose on his forehead. 'My dear man. Wouldn't . . . dream of

33

it. 'S yours.'

He picked it up just the same and peered at it.

'Wait.' He raised a finger and I watched him sway to the phone at the end of the bar and dial the number with deliberation. He spoke for a few seconds, tapping his fag-holder on the receiver, then hung up and walked back to the table setting his bowler carefully on his head.

'And?'

'Answering service. Told them to ring you back here.'

'Me?'

He looked pained. 'Of course. 'S your number n'est ce pas?'

He collected his concentration and walked straight as a die across the club and up the stairs. I ordered another Gilbey's.

Six

It's a mistake to get philosophical too early in the evening. By nine I was still on my tod getting more and more chocker over a bottle of mother's and giving all who came in range the evil eye. It wasn't that I didn't know anybody there – in fact I knew three or four too many, I just didn't fancy any slaps on the back. Funny really, because there I was miserable as sin with the best part of four ton ruining the cut of my jacket and you'd think with that sort of bread a man would need no excuse for a bit of a giggle. However. Scotch's is the sort of place where they're very sensitive to a person's private needs and after a few attempts the word seemed to have got about that I wasn't in the market for laughs that night. I hadn't even got the energy to decide whether to eat or go and sleep it off.

So when Scotch tapped my shoulder I was sitting chin in hand staring at the label. Now it wasn't like Scotch to come the malarky when you'd made it plain you didn't want to know so he must have wanted something pretty bad. I frowned at him.

'Telephone.'

I turned to the bottle. 'You haven't seen me.'

'I told them that. They said it was important.'

'Who?'

'Jake. Something like that. You want me to give him the distance, Harry?'

I scratched my head. The Major? Well you could never tell. 'Hang about.'

The telephone seemed a long way off. I forced myself between a pair of birds nattering over sweet Martinis and stared thoughtfully

35

down the neckline of the one on the left as I picked up the receiver. 'Yeah?' I plugged one ear with my finger to shut out the noise.

'Mr Grant?' The voice was middle-aged London. I yawned, feeling one of the birds pressing close. A brass looking for a fare.

'Right.'

'You called earlier?'

'Right. So I did.'

A pause. 'Well? Enquiries at the number you called can only be in answer to one message.'

'I see.'

'And how can you help me?'

Don't ask. I didn't know what he was on about but the clouds were already starting to part when I remembered Hurly and his percentage.

'Well, I don't know about me personally. Maybe. Depends on the offer.'

'Good. When can we meet?'

'Hang about,' I told him, 'I lead a busy life. What's the offer?'

I could hear him breathe. 'Mr Grant.' The words slowed as he picked through them like mines. 'You have no prior knowledge of me or my clients. We pay our way, you'll have to take my word for that. If we can use you I promise you you will be recompensed.'

'So long as you're an honest man.'

'When can we meet?' His impatience was catching.

'Any time.'

'See me in the Wagner in half an hour. You know the Wagner?'

'Yes.'

'Ask for me.'

I set the phone down careful. One of the birds was giving me the come-on as I leafed through the A–D directory. A few hundred Drakes. Could've been any one of them. I looked at the brass. Her mouth was red and full but though I could hear the sound of her voice I couldn't connect the words into a sentence. I was in two minds. I mean what I really wanted was a good kip and a pose in the sun for a few days, business having developed very nicely thank you but then you never know and who was I to say no to Lady Luck? This time tomorrow I could be sitting here flush, just for the sake of a phone call. I stepped back to the table, put the top on the bottle and slammed it down between the two birds at the bar.

'Best wishes from Uncle Harry.' I was feeling better already.

The Wagner is a Kraut caff in Poland Street where the strudel is like Vader makes and the waiters are the sort that gave Nazism a bad name. I've never had a dinner in the Wagner yet that didn't end with some sort of bother and I've seen the same happen to others so I know it's not just me. Anyway, this time I was prepared to make a special effort. I started off wrong by asking for Drake's table downstairs.

'Drake?' I thought this particular Kraut was going to lay one on me. 'Upstairs.'

So I marched upstairs. The first floor is a barn of a place with off-white walls and a boarded floor crowded with black wood tables and chairs. It was nearly empty, the light bouncing off the starched white table-cloths.

'Drake?' The waiter I spoke to was the image of Martin Bormann in sideburns. 'There.' He pointed to one of the empty tables. I clumped across the boards and scraped out a chair. Then I sat fiddling with the cutlery wondering whether to start a barney by asking for service. In the end I thought better of it and contented myself by tracing lines in the table-cloth with the point of a knife.

Drake was ten minutes late but unmistakable when he did arrive. He was a heavy feller who moved with such care you could tell he would never bounce the baby on its head for fun. He breathed heavily, puffing cheeks purple with too much booze or sun or both, frowning under eyebrows thick as hedges. His suit was stretched round his middle, showing a stranglehold on his crutch. He pulled out a chair and lowered himself like Henry the Fifth in heavy drag. And he stank of the Law.

'Mr Grant.' His hand was pale, resting soft and wet in mine. Still, he had something because within seconds Martin Bormann was poncing about like he'd exhumed the Führer himself. Drake eyed the menu and ran his tongue over a pair of fat lips.

'Yes. Good. I'll have the potato soup followed by . . . eisbein with . . . sauerkraut and dumplings. Are the dumplings fresh?' Martin looked hurt, if you can imagine Martin Bormann looking hurt. Drake raised his eyebrows at me. 'It's on me.'

I gave the first course a miss and settled for a Wienerschnitzel from south of the border so as not to compromise my convictions. Martin skipped away for a couple of lagers and Drake leaned towards me, eyebrows meeting in the middle.

'I like the food here.' He waited for an argument. 'I like German

37

food. I spent some time in Germany, you know. After the War.' He unbuttoned his jacket and the edges snapped open like the shutter on a camera. 'Course, the place was in a right mess in those days. Bombed to smithereens. Amazing what they've done since.'

Well, if he thought I was here to heil the Economic Miracle he was going to be surprised. Martin Bormann brought two pints of lager so I put my glass in my mouth and shut up.

'Course you wouldn't remember much of that,' he told me. 'You a Londoner?' I nodded. 'You don't mind me asking?'

'No.'

He set his pint down and waved a fat hand. 'No. Don't get me wrong. I'm not quizzing you. The less I know in my business the better. Up to a point.'

'You a copper?'

He coughed into his glass and mopped his face with a handkerchief the size of a small table-cloth. 'Why do you ask?'

'You look fuzzy.'

He grinned in a sort of I-don't-like-to-boast fashion. 'Well ... I used to be. Not any more.'

'Why did you stop?' If I'd known I wouldn't have bothered. 'It's a good life, isn't it? Lots of sport and fresh air. And a pension.'

Martin Bormann got between us with a gallon of potato soup. It was the first time I'd seen a bloke tuck his napkin into his shirt collar like a baby in need of a shave. He nearly strangled himself along the way and stopped being friendly.

'Right.' He ladled soup into his mouth. 'I shall tell you as much as you need to know. I'm a private investigator. Twenty years on the force. I retired before I was pensioned off with holes in my boots and a council flat to show for it. I am acting in the present matter for a certain client ... who is prepared to spend a large sum of money ... to see his interests served.' He finished his soup, wiped his mouth and took a swig of lager. 'Now the question is, who will serve his interests best?'

'Are you asking me?' There was a smell of genuine silver about the bloke that was beginning to interest me. He held up a hand.

'Let me finish.' He belched quietly behind his palm. 'Now if I judge you right you are a man that mixes in ... shall I say, varied, company.' I frowned, trying to keep up. 'And among that company ... ah!' Bormann arrived with a hundredweight of eisbein and a schnitzel draped like a cloth over a tray. He piled Drake's plate with sauerkraut, potatoes and dumplings and Drake attacked the mound like a wolf on holiday in the sheepfold. Table manners were not Sergeant Drake's strong point. 'And among the varied company in which you move...' his jaws worked over five pounds of spuds while he pointed his fork at the ceiling, 'you can no doubt call on a number of talents. Talents for sale.' I picked at the schnitzel, waiting for a clue. 'Now,' he shovelled a forkful of pork into his mouth, 'my clients are willing to pay a percentage to anyone bringing about an introduction to the right man. That's where you come in.' He winked. 'It'll be worth your while.'

I put down my knife and fork and scanned him steady and brittle. 'Don't waste my time, Drake.'

He stopped chewing. 'What?'

'I don't run errands.' I snapped my fingers at Martin Bormann and reached for my wallet. 'I just remembered an appointment.'

Drake waved Bormann away. 'Wait.'

'Make it quick.' I was half out of my chair. Drake picked his teeth with a fingernail. His eyes were narrowed and he breathed heavily through his nose. The purple had drained from his cheeks.

'Sit down. Please.'

'You think I talk to coppers for fun?'

'Sit down.'

I sat. Drake cleared his throat. 'We must obviously discuss the matter from a different viewpoint.'

'How much?' My hands were wet.

Drake set his knife and fork together in the gravy. 'A great deal of money, Mr Grant.'

'How much?'

He watched me closely. 'Ten thousand. Five before and five after.'

My pulse rattled in my ears. 'Crap.'

'That's the price, Mr Grant.'

'I don't know your clients and for that sort of money I don't want to know them,' I said. 'Why don't you trot back and tell them the big boys don't play for that kind of money?'

I was on a tightrope. He looked pained. 'I do beg to differ. I know very well it can be achieved for ten thousand.'

I snorted. 'Fifteen. Half down like before.'

Drake was sweating. 'That's a great deal of money.'

I nodded. 'You tell your friends that's the kind of stakes you play when you mix it with the grown-ups.' I clenched my fists under the table. 'Look. I'm a pro, right? I take the chances, I take the rap. I wouldn't stay in business ten minutes if I didn't offer that kind of service. That's why the money's got to be worth it.'

He lapsed quiet while Martin Bormann cleared away the plates and brought the coffee. Drake filled his cup with sugar and stirred it like a man with a lot to think about. 'I shall have to confer with my clients.'

'Do that.'

'You understand there are other candidates?'

I shrugged. 'You'd be a fool not to shop around. But I'll tell you this for nothing. Look for the one that comes dearest.'

We finished coffee and Drake called for the bill.

'Where can I contact you?' I asked.

He wagged a finger like a Frankfurter. 'Leave that to me.'

'Fair enough. You can get me at the same number. Leave a message if I'm out.'

He paid the bill and we left together. 'Keep using the name Grant,' I advised him, 'It'll do for now.'

We stood on the pavement and he seemed to recover some of his old bounce. 'Now . . . a taxi. Can I drop you anywhere?'

'My car's round the corner.'

'I never bring my car into the West End.' He flagged down a cab and got in, pushing the window down. 'I'll be in touch.' He paused. 'Mr Grant. My clients will be suitably grateful towards anyone assisting them to dispose of the particular thorn in their side.' He slammed the door. 'But at your price I can't promise anything.' He fell back in his seat as the cab pulled away from the kerb.

Drake wanted a hit-man.

Seven

When I got back to Fulham I dropped my jacket on the carpet and made straight for the booze on account of my state of mind was not conducive to eight hours' beauty. After a couple or three fast shots of gin I dug Sinatra out of the pile beside the stereo and let him blanket the gaff in swells of sound that blew the cobwebs out of my skull. I lay on the couch then paced the room rearranging bits of furniture, after which I opened the windows and took gulps of warm Wandsworth Bridge air. Drake wanted a hit-man. Not any old villain to put the boot in for five quid but somebody worth at least ten grand by his own admission which of course meant he could be talked up. Ten grand buys you a pro who will take charge of the whole hassle and do it quiet and clean and cause no bother. There weren't many of those about. In fact if the word was true you could count those in London on the fingers of one hand and still be left enough to pick a pocket, and if what Drake had said about other candidates was right he might have found a couple already.

I'll admit that when I rumbled what he wanted I caught a touch of the deaths sufficient to put me on the nearest Jumbo to Vladivostok. You can't afford to pass up many ways of making a score these days but that was one that turned me off quicker than a light in a brass's bedroom and right now every alarm in my body was clanging like a fleet of fuzz-cars raiding a riot. I mean what if they boxed me in when I got the money? My finger on the trigger and hot breath on my neck – Christ, it was unthinkable.

But however you looked at it somebody was ready to drop ten grand. Ten grand. I could feel the noughts trickling through my veins up my arms and clocking up behind my eyes.

At three o'clock I was still pacing the floor sober and red-eyed, picking my way through the empty gin-bottles while Sinatra ground down to hiccups and the noughts in my bloodstream kept me high as a kite in a force ten gale. I lay on the couch and laced my fingers behind my head with eyes shut trying to relax but the thumps in my chest bounced the couch and in minutes I was up again reaching for the bottle and following my feet as they made appointments without permission. I was wearing a path in the carpet and a hole in my stomach until I clamped myself into a chair for a count of fifty.

I woke bolt upright reaching for my wallet through a shaft of sunlight teeming in the windows from over the roofs of the houses opposite. The room stank of gin. My tie had escaped my collar and lay snaked round the empties on the floor. It took a while to come together but the noughts hadn't stopped circulating while I kipped and half of my brain felt like it had stayed up doing algebra by candlelight. My left arm had made a suicide pact with my leg during the night and there was a gnome with a temper trying to break out of my skull. I groped to the kitchen and tried to make a cup of Nescafé, watching the kettle for fully ten minutes while it boiled over the draining board. I tried a slice of toast but couldn't hold it down. It took another half-hour before I climbed into the bath and persuaded my arm to join me. By the time I'd finished shaving things were lining up the way I wanted. Naked, I sat on the couch and phoned Crab.

'You got a radio in the taxi?'

Crab said yes, what for, and I offered him twenty quid to stay tuned in till midnight every day for the next week in case I needed him. We settled on twenty-five and a time limit of five days because Crab could never resist an argument. Then I dressed carefully in my beige mohair.

About eleven-thirty I cleaned out the Stud and coasted up to Frankie's in the Fulham Road. Frankie ran a used car lot, a herd of captive motors fenced in an old bomb site with little flags on the wires. The best motors were lined up near the pavement. Frankie nearly dropped dead when I told him I wanted a conditional part-ex for something less noticeable and I had a bit of bother convincing him I'd pay him twenty quid if I wanted the Stud back inside a week. We settled on thirty and I came away with a five-year-old Mini 1275 and another two ton in my pocket. The Mini had the right sort of zip to shift me quick and the beauty of it was it was no different to a thousand others you see on the street. I drove it up to Scotch's.

The only way Drake could contact me was through Scotch and if that meant camping out there for a week I was ready to do it. Scotch opened at twelve and by that time I was wearing the concrete off the steps. Scotch didn't look surprised.

'Harry? Drop of Gilbey's?'

'Small one.'

If I was going to prop the walls up for a week I did not care to be stoned when my moment came.

By five in the afternoon the whole deal was looking flat and the zig-zags left off for a bit. I borrowed Scotch's *Daily Mirror* and sat in a corner with a sniff of gin wondering when Scotch was going to ask what it was all about because even Scotch is human. Sort of. But like I said Scotch stays in business and out of bother by never asking questions and he wasn't going to bend the rules for me. So I avoided his eye and concentrated on strikes in London and bombs in Belfast and earthquakes in Ecuador. Then there was this bloke that passed himself off as a National Health visitor and toured the council estates telling housewives he'd come to examine them. There was no gelt in it – just a bit of a grope, which makes you wonder about the brains of your average bird when you read how well he got on. Anyway the berk got two years and nobody can tell me any grope is worth that sort of porridge. The place was starting to fill slowly, blokes dropping in with copies of *Sporting Life,* others chatting up their mates and some just scanning the wallpaper. Then a couple of blokes dragged a mark in. I was too far to hear their particular line but it must've been good judging by the quiddies changing hands in the corner. Probably to do with the gee-gees. I once heard of a bloke that stung an American for Nelson's Column, which makes you consider how times have changed since. Half the swedes on the street are working their own cons these days and you've got to watch where you point the nose even if you were born behind the wheel.

Scotch thumped my shoulder. 'Your call.'

I had to grip the receiver in both hands. 'Yeah?'

'Mr Grant? Can we meet?'

'Where?'

'See me in the Conch at seven-thirty.'

I held the buttons down then dialled Crab's operator.

'Tell Crab the Conch, about eight. I'll be with a fat party. He's the fare. Got that?'

I slapped a couple of quid on the bar and ran for the door.

'Mind how you go,' yelled Scotch.

'I was born minding,' I told him.

The Conch is part of the Albemarle Hotel but round the corner away from the main entrance. You walk down a few steps and find yourself under a grass roof in Tahiti staring at boggle-eyed totem poles and Spanish waiters, which is a pity because you'd think they'd hire a few virgins to hump the booze. Never mind, the overall effect is real enough and good for a giggle if you're not Tahitian. Drake was sweating on a log chair next to a pool, contemplating a plastic alligator. The palms and reeds round the pool faded into a painted beach and seascape in the distance with special lights chasing clouds across the Tahitian sky. Drake didn't look at home. He waved me to the opposite chair like Nipper of the Yard come to investigate fertility murders. 'Have a drink.' A waiter brought a menu as big as a newspaper and about as much bother to read only there weren't any photos. Judging by the names they'd invented a picture or two would've come in handy. Stuff called Jungle Night Draught and Headman's Cup. I pointed to Drake's glass in its bamboo cup. 'Some of that.'

'Sir,' the waiter scribbled on his pad and made for the Copra Bar.

'Good stuff.' Drake smacked his lips and tried to get comfortable without falling in the pool. Water trickled over the plastic rocks and Hawaiian music chimed from concealed speakers. 'Trouble is it tastes like cordial and before you know where you are you're on your back in Hanover Square. Good stuff though.' I was getting to like him less and less. 'My wife doesn't drink.' He must've been there longer than I thought. 'Pity. I've often thought a decent drink and a good dinner are among life's biggest pleasures.'

The waiter brought something that was trying to climb out of the bamboo cup, all foaming through a fruit salad and costing ninety pence. Drake folded his hands across his belly and studied me through half-closed eyes. 'Now. I expect you're wondering why you're here.' He sipped his cocktail. 'I am instructed to find out more about you.'

There was a clap of thunder and a tropical storm broke over the pool. Drake shifted his chair with difficulty.

I started to get up. 'You dragged me to this plastic-coated caff just to tell me that?'

He caught my sleeve and scanned the bar like he was scared of something. 'Listen.' He grabbed my wrist. 'If you get the contract my clients will pay the fee you ask.'

'Thanks,' I said. 'What else can you tell me to brighten my day?' I pushed my face close to his. 'Look. We better call it quits. I've thought it over. I don't deal with amateurs.'

His face turned a funny shade but maybe it was the Tahitian lightning ripping the sky apart five feet from his chair.

'Amateurs? If nothing else, Mr Grant, I can assure you my clients are very serious.' I could see the pores in his nose. 'And something else. If you are . . . what you say you are . . . you may be accustomed to, well, I suppose a lot of people would rather see you . . . out of the way, so to speak.' Drake was sweating and I let him squirm in my gaze. 'My clients . . . well, this is a genuine enquiry, I can't say better than that. For that reason I have to ask you a few questions.'

I fidgeted. 'Forget it. I don't provide answers.'

His colour was returning to normal. 'Understandable. But bear with me please.' He took a swig of the stuff at his elbow. 'When did you last work?'

'I don't need to work often.'

'I believe that. When was the last time?'

I scanned him long and cool. 'A year ago.'

'And where was that?' The storm was easing off and the sun was coming out all over the plastic alligators. I just sat there watching him till he looked away. 'Very well.' He scratched the side of his nose. 'Any . . . preferred techniques?'

I smiled thin and bitter. 'I don't leave trademarks.'

Drake's job must've been getting him down because he almost shuddered. 'Good.'

'Look.' I stabbed a finger towards him. 'If you don't know that a pro can't be traced you and your friends are wasting your time.' I yawned. 'Why don't you drop in down Mile End? You'd find a hundred who'd do it for a tenner. They're more your class.'

I'd swear Drake almost smiled to himself. 'I had to ask.'

Maybe he knew more about it than he let on. I was getting the zig-zags again. He frowned into his drink. 'This contract a year ago. Did it take you abroad?' I sat it out. 'Take you long?'

I dropped the fruit salad in the ashtray and raised the cup, watching him over the rim. 'I always take long.'

'How long?'

'If you're thinking of setting a schedule forget it. I work at my own pace.'

He wanted to believe me. 'Of course. You won't find my clients difficult.' He loosened his tie and the flesh on his neck slipped under his collar.

'Some contracts,' I said slowly, 'can take twelve months.' He waited. 'I need to get the feel of the location as well as the mark.'

'I'm sure.' He raised a hand to the waiter as casual as if he was enjoying a natter with an old friend. 'Another?' I shook my head and he ordered another concoction for himself. 'What do you do, for instance, in a place where English isn't spoken?'

Christ, it looked like I was going to have to travel for my fifteen grand. 'I make out.'

It came to me as I watched him gulp his drink. 'Some places are foreign even if they are English spoken.' I shrugged. 'Like America.'

He looked so innocent I couldn't be sure he'd picked it up. 'I know what you mean.' The waiter brought his cocktail and Drake had trouble reaching the change in his trouser pocket. He sat back puffing. 'Not that I've been there of course.'

I showed him how carefully I was relaxing. 'It's a few years since I was there.'

Drake stirred his drink with a nine-inch plastic spoon. 'Like it?'

I looked back hard. 'So-so.'

He tried to recapture the almost matey feel he'd worked to produce. 'Of course. I'm told some parts are very European in feeling.'

If he'd watched he would've seen my hands shaking. I was deliberately casual, even smiling a little. 'That's the north-east.'

'And the rest?' He watched intently.

I yawned. 'Texas is a good place. There's no English town like Houston, say, or Dallas.' I blinked and gave him the freeze with my eyes. 'You ask too many questions, copper.'

He flinched and sat back in his chair cradling his glass in his hands, pudgy fingers sliding over the condensation. 'It's my job.'

I set my drink down. 'You ask a lotta questions and don't make with any answers yourself. Where's the contract? I mean, what country?'

He gazed at the pool. 'Here. London.'

46

I looked at my watch. 'I've got other fish to fry right now. You're taking up too much of my time.'

He heaved out of his chair and had a go at adjusting his waistband, which was unsuccessful on account of his trousers being three sizes too small. If he didn't watch where he put his feet he'd smash the table to matchwood. Suddenly we were surrounded by waiters dusting us down and wishing us goodbye and goodnight and chucking the remains of my fruit salad to the plastic alligators.

We stood on the pavement.

'Let me know,' I said.

Crab was right on target, hire light and all twenty yards down the road. Just to make sure I raised my hand but Drake was ahead of me greedy and wanting to get away. He pretended manners. 'Sorry. Are you taking a taxi?'

'Forget it.' I frowned.

He looked relieved. 'I'll call you.'

Crab, hair plastered down like skin, clocked up a few extras on the meter as he accelerated away.

I was humming as I walked through Hanover Square.

Eight

I was relaxing in my pink linen suit and plum shirt while I sipped a light ale at a table on the terrace of the Serpentine and contemplated my past and more importantly my future, which by now had assumed uncertain aspect. It being Sunday evening the pub was hot and crowded with swedes and other colonials from Kensington and was consequently no place for meditation. In fact another five minutes would have seen me chewing the carpet. But it was cool outside and peopled only by quiet clumps of Nigels drinking Babycham and giving no bother except they blocked my view of the lake which had turned solid when the sun slipped behind the trees. I was deep in thought when a hand fell on my shoulder and caused me to leap three feet off my chair.

'Don't do that!'

Crab looked shocked. 'Sorry Harry. No offence.'

I shot my cuffs and straightened my tie. 'None taken.' I watched him shift from one foot to the other. 'You're a bag of nerves, straight up. Have a drink.'

I fought through the mob and got him a Guinness just to show no ill-will. He was perched on a chair when I got back. 'So what's the story?'

He tore a page from a notebook and slid it across the table. 'Camden High Street. First floor. Name of Mason and Coburn.' He swallowed a mouthful of Guinness. 'Cheers.'

I put the page in my wallet. 'You done well old son. Now how much did we say?'

He crossed and uncrossed his legs. 'Twenty-five.'

I knew if I didn't give him an argument he'd think he'd let me off light. 'No, come on. That was when we thought you'd have to hang about for a week or more. How much for half a day?'

''Kinell,' Crab went pink, 'you do your mate a favour and what do you get? Bleeding aggro. Twenty-five.'

'Now look . . .'

His eyes sparked with the fun of it all. 'Look yourself.' He put down his Guinness and stabbed a finger at me. 'You know me, Harry. Father Bloody Christmas. I'd do it for free; in fact I am doing it for free, I'm just charging expenses. There's diesel, oil, tyres, all that as well as the fares I lost. I can't do fairer than twenty-five, now, can I?'

I reached into my pocket. 'My life, if I had your job.' I counted out twenty-five. 'There. Break my heart. Take it.'

He stuffed the cash in his pocket and we both relaxed.

'What's this job about, then, Harry?' I wished he wouldn't drum his fingers on the table. He'd got so he didn't realize he was doing it, poised in his dark suit and stiff collar, nails bitten down to the knuckles, tapping away. I yawned and scanned the lake.

'Oh, some berk I've gotta keep an eye on.'

Crab sniffed a score. 'Need any help? I mean I'm always available.'

'Can't afford you.'

'No, seriously.' He smoothed his hair back. 'You need a minder or anything just ask, all right?'

'I'll bear it in mind.'

We sat quiet over our drinks while the light faded and the citizens grew silent and romantic staring at the water. It was that peaceful I could've pushed the whole business out of my mind and carried on scoring a quiet quid or two up West forever. Jesus, just the thought of cold steel in my hands was enough to start the banshees baying. But I knew come morning the thought of that fifteen grand would nag and I'd never forgive myself for passing up the chance.

'Want another, Harry?' Crab drained his Guinness.

I looked at my watch and stood up. 'No ta. Better make a move.'

We crossed the terrace and made our way to the road where I'd parked the Mini.

'Bloody hell,' said Crab. 'What happened to your motor?'

'Sawed in half,' I told him. 'Mind how you go.'

I did a U-turn and drove back north.

The Cypriots and the Irish did a merger to nick Camden High Street off the English and I reckon the English were double chuffed to let

49

it go. It's still grimy and the motors still use it like Silverstone on the way to Golders Green but these days shops selling peppers and olives are mixed with boozers that spit Micks on a Saturday night like shot from a gun, and black-shawled hags have a knees-up every Sunday by way of preparation for Judgement Day. Of course Marks and Spencer and the Co-op put you straight.

It was nearly dark when I drove past Drake's place, parked the Mini by the kerb a hundred yards up the street, and walked back to do a proper scan. The ground floor was occupied by a telly showroom with televisions stacked like egg-boxes chuntering away to themselves in the window, which was lucky because it allowed me to latch on to the clump of Micks watching the show from the pavement. It can't be bad watching fifty telly sets at once when you're pissed out of your head which was why most of them were swaying with the strain and didn't notice me. I had a sniff round the doorway beside the showroom and saw Mason and Coburn's plate outside with a couple of others. There was no bell so I supposed the door stood open during the day. The plates said there was a dentist on the second floor and a tax consultant on the third. Nobody living there. I doddled round the block and had a gander at the back. His rear windows looked direct into a builder's yard and I began to cheer up. If I was a builder I'd watch my stock but lucky for me most builders don't. The row of houses opposite were empty, plastered with notices about redevelopment, and the nearest streetlamp spilled orange over the pavement about twenty yards away. The wall in front was about eight feet high with a pair of gates rotting at the bottom and leaning in different directions, held at the middle by an old padlock. I could just see the remains of broken glass set in the top of the wall, worn smooth by weather, and four lamp-holders stood like soldiers looking down the brickwork on the street side. They hadn't worked for years.

I sat in the Mini for a bit and had a think. I could do the building, no bother. But Drake might have kept his stuff in a peter and though I'd had practice as a kid with doors and windows a peter was not my line of country. For that I needed someone special. Like Angel Horrocks.

Angel's caff looked worse than ever in electric light, showing the holes in the lino and the dirt in the corners. Angel's missus wasn't frying the chips, which might have explained the number of customers, but the biddy doing the cooking could easily have been her mum. I slipped past while she was sticking her nose in the pan and ran upstairs. Angel must've finished a game not long since because the door to the cardroom was open, the window was wide and his missus was dropping ash as fast as she was sweeping it up.

'Game's finished, dear.'

'I know. I come to see Angel.'

Her fag glowed. 'Wotcher want?' She coughed.

'Nothing, Missus. Just a chat.'

She hobbled close, holding her back. She must've been twelve inches shorter than me. 'What about?'

'Well to tell the truth, darlin, I wondered if he'd thought of selling you. I sense a feeling between us, a comradeship so deep it is almost sexual in its profundity.' I pinched her cheek and she ducked like a flyweight.

'Cheeky young sod.' She poked me with the broomhandle. 'He's in the front room.'

Angel was sitting in his vest and Y-fronts watching a telly western. Y-fronts like tents I had never seen before and I wondered if he got them made special.

'Who's your tailor, then, Ducky?'

He looked pleased. 'Hullo Harry boy. Get yourself a glass.' His thighs rasped as he waddled to the tin of Watneys in the corner. I rescued the cleanest glass and he held the tin in both hands while he poured.

'Angel.' I blew the foam flat. 'How are you fixed for a little job?'

A ripple started in Angel's belly and wobbled all the way to his ankles. He tip-toed to the door, closed it so the latch didn't click, then turned up the telly. Blokes in hats were pointing shooters at each other.

'What sort of job?'

'Drop of B and E. Probably a peter to blow.'

He looked doubtful. 'Dunno. You know me, Harry. Best peter-man in the business at one time. But I haven't done a peter in five years, not since my last drop of porridge.' He scanned the door, all anxious. 'And I promised Ma no more bother with the Law.'

I patted his hand. 'Angel my old dear, she need never know. A nice clean break. Quiet, simple, no aggro. You can be back for breakfast.' I thought a bit. 'Tell you something else. You can have it all.'

Angel was amazed. 'What's in it for you?'

'Information. That's all I want. A bit of paper. A file maybe.'

51

'How d'you know it'll be in the peter?'

'I don't, do I?' I sipped warm Watneys. 'I'm asking you in case it is. Either way you bust the peter and pocket the pickings.'

'Where?'

'Camden Town.'

'What's the pitch?'

This was going to get bothersome. 'An office.'

'Whose?'

'Belongs to a PD.'

Angel made a rude noise. 'You've gotta be joking. What's he got, a stainless Timex and fifty LVs?'

I ran a finger round the rim of my glass. 'I don't know, not till I get there.'

Angel picked his toes. 'Well, you go and see. Then come back and tell me and I'll let you know.'

I leaned along the couch. 'Look. A PD often keeps valuables for clients. Sometimes he's paid in cash too, by yobs keeping it quiet from the Law. There might be a couple of grand stashed there.'

'Might be.' Angel nodded on his chins. 'You go and see.'

I started walking up and down. 'Alright. You want to be sure of a few readies.'

Angel filled his glass. 'You could say I might be persuaded by a few readies. Yes.'

'So how much would you normally expect to clear once you've split with the driver and the minder and Uncle Tom Cobbleigh and all?'

You could tell when Angel was trying to think because his forehead creased and he took on a very bothered look. 'I never come out of a job yet with less than a hundred nicker, but I wouldn't bother myself for that much. Two hundred minimum.'

I took a deep breath. 'Tell you what I'll do for you. I'll guarantee you two hundred. Personally. If there's two hundred or more in the peter you keep it all and get nothing from me. Less than two hundred and I'll make up the difference.'

Angel gnawed his thumb-nail. 'You really want that file, don't you Harry?'

'Yes I really do.' I glanced at the telly. 'Is it a deal?'

He scratched his jaw. 'I dunno. Christ, Harry, I haven't done a peter in years. It's your technology that changes, not the peterman. You got to keep abreast of the times in this job, you know.

They've probably got peters these days I never even heard of. Suppose I can't bust it?'

I wasn't feeling happy but I grinned. 'You know your trouble?'

'What?'

'Confidence. You got no confidence.' I finished off the Watneys. It was really warm at the bottom. 'If you don't bust it I'll give you a hundred anyway. How's that?'

Angel put his hand under his vest and patted his belly. 'You never give up, do you?' He puffed out his cheeks. 'I don't suppose you know anything about this peter? I mean, does it need blowing or can it be cut or picked?' He held up a hand. 'Forget it. Blowing's fastest but I couldn't lay hands on the jelly in time.' He grumbled. 'Suppose I'll have to look out all my old gear again.'

I held out a hand. 'Good for you.'

His missus came in as we shook hands. 'Whispers tell lies,' she cackled. 'What's the telly doing on so loud?' She dragged her broom across the carpet and turned the volume down while Angel started a punch-up with his trousers.

'I'll just see Harry out, Ma.'

'Already?'

''Fraid so,' I said. 'He doesn't trust me in your company.' I blew her a kiss. 'I don't trust myself.'

She shook the broom at me and bits fell all over the couch.

Angel stopped at the caff door. 'When?'

'Tomorrow night.' I thought. 'There's a high wall with glass on top.'

He nodded. 'Should be all right.'

'Good. I'll pick you up at two. I'll be in a Mini.'

'See you.'

Sergeant Drake had bitten off more than he could chew this time.

Nine

Angel's caff was blind but the Chinamen were still about at two in the morning doing deals and swopping chat and not behaving inscrutable at all, which was disappointing at that time of night. I coasted up to the kerb, switched the lights out and pretended to be looking for something under the dash so I wouldn't get scanned too close by passers-by. In a few seconds Angel slipped out of the caff carrying a sort of oversized black carpet-bag and fishing tackle. He was wearing a light sports jacket as big as a bedspread. I opened the door and he wrestled with his gear, finally shoving it into the back after clobbering me twice on the head and knocking the mirror out of line. Then he tried to get to the front, cussed horribly, got out, adjusted the seat and finally wedged himself in with his knees up around his chin. He looked pissed off. 'Where's your bloody car?'

'It shrank at the cleaners,' I told him, 'and if you think I'm going anywhere with you in that jacket you're crazy.'

Angel sneered. 'You great berk. What d'you reckon the Law would make of a bloke in black like you carrying a black bag?'

He had a point. 'What's all that fishing tackle then?'

He mumbled. 'Ma thinks we're going to Southend on a fishing trip.' I nearly wrapped the Mini round a lamp-post. We were silent for the rest of the trip but the air was so tight a hand-clap would have had us both off the ground and running for cover.

Camden Town was quiet apart from the late-nighters thundering up the High Street in their Volvos. I turned west off the main road and into Arlington Road, drifting to a stop just outside the builder's yard.

Angel glanced both ways, opened the car door and humped his bag half out of the car. He took off his jacket and bundled it in the back, then rummaged in the bag and pulled out a long nylon rope attached to a grappling iron. Last came a blanket. He tied up the bag and looked both ways again.

'Right. Put the car further down.'

He dropped his clobber at the foot of the wall while I coasted further down the street, stuffed a pair of gloves in my pocket, locked the car and ran back. Without his jacket I could hardly see him at five yards. Like I've said, when Angel was excited he moved fast. He folded the blanket lengthways and tossed it so it hung over the top of the wall. Then, stepping back a pace, he swung the rope and let go. The iron glinted in the air and clanged as it bit into the old brick on the other side. Angel took up the slack and was astride the wall in one fast move. He held out his hand for the bag. I passed it up and he dropped it into the yard. 'Come.' I hauled myself up. The blanket masked the worn glass on the top and I sat still measuring the drop. The yard was paved and I bruised my knee on the slabs. 'OK.' Angel's shadow loomed, poised, and dropped, amazingly light beside me. He released the iron and drew the rope and blanket down with a tug. I picked up the blanket while he coiled the rope.

The dog, crafty as an Arab, must've waited till we were both down before pulling the trigger because the first I knew was a ton of fur teeth and claws had hit me in the chest and started ripping at my throat. I fell against the wall, holding him off with the blanket round my arm. The horrible part was the silence, not even a snarl. I yelled, trying to keep the blanket between me and the teeth at my face. 'Over his head!' hissed Angel. 'The blanket!' Somehow I got a hold on the dirty fur at its chest with my free hand, elbow wedged against the wall, holding it just clear of my face. My arm trembled with the strain. A couple of false starts with the blanket, then over its head. It didn't make much difference. The blanket was alive, punching, wrenching and stretching with the force inside. The iron flashed. Angel aimed for the head. And again. Again. The madness slowed. Angel hit him once more. The bundle relaxed and felt heavy. The dog slipped out onto the paving, twitched and lay still.

We stepped back heaving like a pair of locomotives.

'Christ.' Angel looked ready to die. I squatted next to the dog with my head in my arms trying to catch breath. The sleeve of my sweater dangled in strips of wool and I could feel blood trickling down my face. It was ten minutes before we moved.

The yard was stacked with bricks arranged in cubes and laid out like houses on a council estate. We moved between the rows towards the wall at the back. The wall was no problem and a couple of minutes after we stood in the dark of Drake's backyard. Like a million others the old house was built with a closet wing extending to the back boundary leaving a quarter of the site free for light and air. Pipes draped the brickwork. Angel scanned the window to the first-floor carsie. 'That'll do.' He put on his gloves and took a jemmy out of his bag. Taking hold of the drainpipe in the corner he placed his feet square against the wall. 'Come when I call you.' I watched him shin up, the jemmy dangling from his waistband, and set his arse against the cill of the window in the corner while his feet pressed one above the other on the pipe. I could hear him breathing as he worried away at the carsie window. A snap. He worked the window open quietly. He heaved himself off the cill got a hand on each jamb and disappeared head first. The rope snaked down. 'Bag first.' I tied the bag on the end of the rope and he hauled it up. The rope dropped again. 'Climb.' It was easier than shinning up pipes. I got my elbows on the cill and fell near the bog, which at that level stank very bad. We sorted ourselves out. 'Put your gloves on.' Angel wiped his handkerchief round the cill and jambs and shut the window.

The carsie door opened onto a stair landing. The balustrade groaned like an old bed as we shuffled down half a flight to what must have been Drake's office. Angel flashed a torch on the lock. He chortled. 'Yale.' He fumbled in his pocket and waved a six-inch bit of celluloid. In fifteen seconds we were standing in the outer office.

There was a desk in front of the window on which stood the shape of a covered typewriter and a two-line switchboard. The far wall was a wooden partition with a half-glazed door marked private. Two filing cabinets leaned against the back wall on the left of the entrance. I opened the door in the partition. Drake's desk was in the same position as his secretary's in the other room so that he too sat with his back to the window. But he had a carpet and one of those high-backed club chairs to suit his size. A couple of easy chairs were drawn up facing the desk and a small table was pushed against the partition carrying a vase of plastic roses. And in the corner, the peter.

Angel nearly clapped his hands.

56

'What?' I asked.

'Old combination. Easy as pie.'

'No cutting?'

He shook his head. 'Leave it to me. We'll have it wide inside an hour.' He spread the blanket on the floor in front of the peter, hauled his bag over and rolled up his sleeves. I started on the filing cabinets in the outer office. There was no sense in disturbing them more than was absolutely necessary. This had to look like an ordinary B and E and Drake must not suss what we'd really come for. No ordinary tea-leaf would waste his time on filing cabinets. And if the file was in the peter it would have to be left as if the peter-man was after nothing but lolly.

As you might have expected the files were stored in alphabetical order based on clients' names. The bottom drawer started at Y and worked back through the alphabet. A good portion of them were old divorce cases – some of them years old – and I wondered how the new divorce laws had knocked his business. The papers were clipped into cardboard folders which were dropped into fixed wallets and I found the best way was to lift each folder in turn, flip through the papers and put it back in its wallet before hitting the next one. This went on for over an hour and I was getting pissed off, down to D in the second drawer and getting certain I wasn't going to find what I'd come for. Angel loomed in the doorway, silhouetted against the light from a street-lamp. I couldn't see his face but his voice was smug. 'Done.' I left a mark in my place and joined him at the peter. It was three-thirty, and in half an hour we had to start worrying about daylight.

Angel's tools were laid out neat on the blanket and the peter door stood open. 'It was a doddle,' said Angel. He shone the torch inside the peter. It wasn't very exciting. A pile of legal-looking documents tied with tape, a fat envelope standing up at the back, a set of old drawings and two wads of tenners in a steel tray. Angel picked them out and counted them with the practised fingers of a bank teller. 'A hundred and eighty.' As he dropped them in his bag I wondered if he'd lifted any before he called me. Not that I didn't trust him. I looked through the rest of the papers. Not only was there no file, I owed Angel twenty quid. I left him to it and went on through the cabinets outside. Twenty minutes proved I was wasting my time. Angel was breathing down my neck. 'Come on. Getting late.'

'Piss off.'

He was right. I could already see the room more clearly. I searched quickly through the drawers in the secretary's desk. A back issue of *Over 21*, make-up, the petty-cash box and a wad of luncheon vouchers. I gave the petty-cash box to Angel. 'Keep it.' Anything that cut down my debts was welcome. He stuffed it in his bag and started moving from one foot to the other. The drawers in Drake's desk were locked. 'Angel!' He scanned the desk. 'Take too long.' He looked at his watch.

'Then bust it!'

He looked at me in the gloom and knew I wasn't joking. I grabbed the jemmy and shoved it into his hands. He knelt beside the desk, scraped at the top of the drawers, tensed, and gave a quick heave. The drawers cracked. 'Hurry, for Chrissake.' He was packing his tools. I chucked out a stainless-steel clock. 'Take it!'

'Don't want it.'

'Take it!' He did as I said. I fumbled through half-a-dozen new files. The third one was what it was all about.

It was a cardboard folder like the ones in the cabinets. On the cover written in ink was the word: 'Carson.' Inside were two loose sheets of lined foolscap. On the first was scribbled: 'L. Carson' underlined twice, then: '23 Vista Villas, Highgate W. Hill.' And in pencil on the right of the address, circled several times: '4 p.m. 17th.' The second page had a list of names:

'J. Cain
Largo
H. Grant.'

The office was getting light and Angel was sweating near the door. 'Come on!' I stared long and hard at the pages, closed the file and dropped it back where I'd found it. We scanned the office. I scattered a few documents on the floor and lifted a barometer off the top of the peter. We left the way we came.

Outside you could already hear the lorries on the High Street. The dog lay at the foot of the wall. Angel scaled the brickwork, had a quick look and helped me over. We dropped into Arlington Road, chucked our clobber in the car and drove south like a bullet. The only bit of light relief that night was calling in at Billingsgate to buy three mackerel for Angel's missus. By five-thirty I'd dropped him at the caff and by six-thirty I was in bed memorizing the words in Drake's file.

Ten

I stumbled out of bed and grabbed the phone.

'Harry?' Scotch. 'Message for you. Tried to get you last night.'

I was waking up fast. 'What is it?'

'This Drake again. He said to tell you forget it. You haven't got the job.' I sat on the bed.

'Harry? You still there?'

'Yes.' I was trying to think. 'Thanks.'

Largo. Cain. Grant. Well, I knew who it wasn't.

I paced the carpet and made a cup of Nescafé. Jesus Largo hadn't caused me another thought since the night he wanted to carve me, but now I started thinking and they were not joyful thoughts. I knew nothing about him but what I guessed was enough to have me dive for cover when I heard his voice. He was the type that did it for pleasure and if it comes to a choice between them that do it for profit and them that do it for fun I knew who I'd rather take home to Mum. It would not have amazed me to find him making the hit for nothing, for the sheer joy of slipping the carver into another warm belly. And he wouldn't have had bother convincing Drake. The distant sound of his eyes blinking told you all you wanted to know about Largo.

Cain.

The word curled in my gut. I knew the name. A whisper. A hiss on the air. Where?

I shook free. The seventeenth was two days away and I'd got to make a start. I only wished the start-line wasn't called Largo. I didn't even know where to look for him.

About one I called Angel to find out what he'd made on the night's business. He'd reckoned up one hundred and eighty-five pounds fifty-five pence with the petty cash but seeing I was an old mate was ready to forget the forty-five pence so I ran down there in the afternoon with the boodle. I had to call him out of a game to pay his dues and it was when I was walking out through the caff I remembered seeing Hurly through the crack in the upstairs door. Hurly.

I sat down at one of the tables near the caff door.

'Didn't catch nothing then?' Angel's missus wiped the Formica with an old vest.

'What?'

'Southend.' She dropped fag ash on the table.

I was quick. 'Three mackerel.'

'That was Dad. He told me you didn't get nothing.'

'Right.'

'Wotcher want?'

'Eh?'

She sighed impatiently. 'Sausage egg-chips bacon egg-chips pie-chips.'

'Oh. Just a cuppa tea, Ma.'

She shuffled to the counter and brought back a nasty liquid in a Pyrex cup chipped round the rim.

'Five pee. Now.'

I paid and tried not to look at the stuff in the cup.

The door at the back opened and a couple of blokes came out shouting cheerio. Hurly slouched through a couple of minutes later and walked right past my table. That solved the problem with the tea. I followed him into the street. He was walking quite straight, cutting through the groups of Chinese and dodging the traffic, obviously sure about his direction. He turned left up an alley towards Shaftesbury Avenue and since that seemed a better chance than most I ran and caught him about half-way. He jumped like a rabbit and showed a face twisted with fright.

'Oh.' He looked sly. 'It's you.'

'Hang about, Boyo,' I grinned, 'I wanna talk to you.'

He tried to push past. 'Some other – '

'Hurly.' I had my arm wedged across the alley. 'You have got something I want.'

He started to talk fast, glancing over my shoulder every fourth word. 'Look now, if it's about the telephone number I can explain . . .

well, Mr Grant, if a man like yourself found himself in my unenviable position what would he have done? There I was, sure in me own mind of a massive win with nothing about me to put on it – '

'Listen, you nasty little Mick.' I raised my other arm and held him trapped. 'I don't mind your lot coming over here taking the bread out of English mouths. I don't even mind when they start chucking bombs in railway stations. But when they try and con me ... Hurly, I get uptight. Know what I mean? What I'm saying is you sold me a pup. That number was already spoken for.'

He twisted his head till his hat fell off. I placed my heel lightly on the crown. 'That was a mistake, Mr Grant, it was all a terrible mistake.'

'Too right.' I ground my shoe into his hat.

'Holy Mary!' He bust out, 'will you stop that?'

I shook my head sadly. 'I know who you sold it to.' I watched his face. 'Hurly ... he is not a nice man.' He flinched as I patted his cheek. 'I am surprised that you keep such company, you know?' His hands fluttered. 'Not by choice Mr Grant, you know who I count as my friends ...'

I sighed into his face. 'I'm an easy-going bloke, Hurly, you know that, don't you?' He nodded so hard his head wobbled dangerously. 'And I will say I don't mind too much, you flogging phone numbers around the manor. You know me. Mad one minute, forgotten the next. But that feller ...' I looked sad for him. 'Well, I'm bloody glad I shan't be in your shoes when he finds out you crossed him.'

I kicked Hurly's hat towards a pile of dustbins. A rat must've thought the catcher called its name because it bust through the rubbish and streaked the length of the alley like a dart.

'How ... would he discover such a thing?' Hurly's question was weak with the answer. I just laughed. At last Hurly twigged his only chance. 'What is it you want?' He was staring at the ground. 'Christ,' I lowered my voice. 'I've heard some horrible things about Largo. He once caught some poor sod making it with his bird. You know what he did?' I shook my head in disbelief. 'But then that was only a rumour. Rumours don't mean a thing, do they Hurly?'

Hurly squeaked. 'What is it you want?' I inspected the lines that had developed on his face during the last few minutes.

'Hurly ...' I sounded interested, 'I shan't be amazed to find your fingers stuffed one by one up some drainpipe, know what I mean?'

Hurly's eyes closed and his shoulders drooped. 'Enough.' His face was a sort of grey colour.

'Where do I find him?'

His eyes bulged. 'Mother of God, not that!'

I shrugged and let him go. 'You know the choice.'

'I don't know, honestly I don't know, Mr Grant. If I could help you I would. I heard he was away for a couple of days.' Hurly was dribbling from the corner of his mouth.

'What about the bird? Kara?'

'As true as God, I don't know!'

I sighed and fetched his hat from the dustbins. 'OK, Hurly. You made your bed.' I jammed the hat down on his ears. 'Take care now. If I was you I'd start thinking about the next ferry to Cork.' I turned towards the end of the alley.

'Mr Grant!' He ran after me, clutching my sleeve. 'I don't know where he lives, honest to God. But his woman used to work as a croupier at Jericho's. That's all I know, I swear on my father's life.'

'Which one?' I nodded. 'Remember what I said, now.' I left him trying to straighten his hat.

Jericho's is a spit and a whistle from Ronnie Scott's. The doors were open when I got there but a couple of chairs blocked the way to tell you the night hadn't yet started. I stepped over them into a reception area all done up with chandeliers like the movies. The mouldings on the walls were picked out in gold paint, giving the place a touch of real class. There was a counter on the left where they took your hat and coat and a pair of doors in the end wall that might have been nicked from Balmoral, draped with blue silk curtains. I took hold of a bronze handle as thick as your arm and pushed through into the gaming room. There was a table for everything; card tables, dice tables, roulette tables – even what might've been two snooker tables in the far corner. The furniture was dark wood carved to look antique, especially the chairs. Great velvet shades hung low over the tables and the roulette boards were spattered with chips. On one side was a sort of gilt cage where you cashed your winnings or bought your chips, and facing it was the bar, about thirty feet long, crusted with gold. In the middle of the ceiling hung the biggest fanciest cut-glass chandelier I've ever seen and painted all over the ceiling was a massive scene of naked birds and cupids all drifting round a load of clouds pointing to the middle. A couple of blokes in shirt-sleeves were sweeping up, and an old woman was polishing glasses behind the bar.

One of the cleaners saw me and stepped up smartish.

'Nine o'clock, John.' He wasn't friendly.

'I know.' I gave him a chance to appreciate my straight white teeth. 'I was looking for somebody.'

'He isn't here.' He started muscling me towards the door.

'She,' I told him.

'Sorry.' He leaned harder. A bird came out from the back in jeans and a sweater. She was carrying a bundle of black satin which I took to be her costume.

'Excuse me.'

She stopped and scanned the heavy, then me, then back again.

'I'm looking for Kara.'

'Kara?' She also had straight white teeth. 'She left six months ago.'

'Come on, John.' Muscles was a bit thick. I shook him off. 'Can't you see I'm rabbiting to a lady?'

He scratched his chin. 'You wanna talk to him, Angie?'

Angie nodded. 'Just a moment, Corby.'

Corby stepped back and watched like he thought we'd lift the takings.

'She left, you said?'

'Some time ago.'

'Look,' I smiled, 'I've got a message for her. It's quite important. Can you tell me where she lives?'

Angie tapped her teeth with a scarlet fingernail. 'I think I can. I once went to a party at her place.' She frowned, playing with a lock of hair. 'Um. Redcliffe Square. Earl's Court. Number ... I don't know whether it was 212 or 221. One of those.'

I raised a hand. 'You've been a great help, Angie baby.'

Her hair fell across her face when she smiled because she inclined her head. 'Any time.'

I made a note of Angie as I passed through the Balmoral doors with Corby breathing down my neck. I turned on the pavement. 'Keep loading the dice, Muscles.'

He spat.

Redcliffe Square must've been a double-posh manor in Victorian times, bloody great six-storey houses all round the sides with pillars and mouldings hung on like icing sugar. These days the old houses are split into bedsits full of Australians but you've still got the green in the middle even if you can't get at it. I rang the housekeeper's bell at 221. She took five minutes to get to the door, puffing like a whale. 'No vacancies.'

'I know, my love. I was looking for a girl. Kara something.'

The old bird undid the scarf round her hair and set about knotting it tighter. 'Kara? Nobody here by that name.'

'A black girl. You remember.'

Something like light sparked in her eyes. 'The black one. Yes. She's gone. Left two months ago.'

'Got a forwarding address, dear?'

She gave me the distance.

'It's OK,' I said, 'I'm a friend of her cousin. He asked me to look her up.'

She thought about that. 'Come in.'

I followed her down to the basement and waited in the lobby outside her gaff. The place smelled of cats and the carpet was in a bad state. When she came back she'd balanced a pair of specs on her nose.

'Forwarding address. She went to live with her brother.' She held the book up to the light. 'See if you can read it.'

I jotted down the address. 'Her brother? D'you know which one? There's two in England. I mean was he short and fat or was he tall with a bald head?'

'That's him,' she said. 'Always in dark glasses on account of trouble with his eyes.'

I felt my face set like concrete. 'Thanks missus.'

'No business messing with black girls,' she muttered as I climbed the stairs. 'No sense of decency.'

The address was in Cornwall Gardens.

Eleven

Cornwall Gardens is something like Redcliffe Square only quieter on account of there is no through road taking up one side. It leads off the west side of Gloucester Road and although you can drive out the opposite side the trees in the middle give it the feeling of a sort of square. Of course, like Redcliffe Square the quality of the houses has gone off during the last ninety years and although the gardens don't see that many Australians the houses are still split into flats for which they charge anything up to a hundred quid a week. Jesus must have been doing nicely, and I wondered what charity he belonged to. Junk probably. None of your grass either, by the look of things.

The address was about half-way along and Largo's flat turned out to be on the ground floor with a bay window divided into three like the rest. I parked across the square for a bit and had a good scan because it looked like I was in for another touch of B and E – alone this time – and I wanted a clear picture before clumping my size nines all over his fur rugs. The front door had two panels of stained glass and looked permanently locked. While I watched somebody came home and let himself in with a key. It was getting dark and several windows were already showing a light but the ground floor bay was dark with the curtains pulled tight so it looked like Hurly might be right for once. Right or not it had to be done and if Hurly was wrong I needed a clear exit. The house had a basement which opened into a light-well fenced off from the pavement by a line of railings and I reckoned a fit man could just about make the jump from the bay to the pavement. If he was very fit. I was feeling tired and what bothered me most was there just wasn't time to make a proper job of it. I drove back to Fulham to wait.

Round three a.m. I parked the Mini near Gloucester Road station and got my gear together. Masking tape, torch, small hammer and a credit card I'd picked up somewhere and never used. Cornwall Gardens was deserted and the cars lined the pavement nose to tail waiting for the morning call. There'd been a drop of rain early in the evening and the street glistened like it was wrapped tight in cellophane. I reached the house, had a quick look up and down and took the stairs to the front door two at a time. When you're doing a house that exposed you can't afford to hang about so I'd come prepared with the tape already cut into six lengths, first a square then two diagonals stuck over the stained-glass panel nearest the lock. My hands were shaking as I folded a handkerchief in the centre of the cross and gave a quick tap with the hammer. Those bloody Victorians knew how to cast glass. It didn't budge. I hit it again and the square gave way under my fingers, fragments stuck to the tape. I eased the glass out quiet and gentle, set it down on the step and felt inside the door for the latch. The door swung inwards. I scooped the glass off the step, laid it on the hall floor and clicked the door shut.

I sat on my panic for a bit, waiting for my eyes to adjust to the dark. A staircase rose from the back and I could pick out the diamond-shaped tiles on the floor. Largo's door led off the hall, framed in heavy wood. I scanned the lock with the torch. Night latch. The credit card slipped into the crack – Christ, I couldn't find the latch. I pressed the card deep as I dared and slid it up and down. Nothing. Sweat was running into my eyes as fast as I could wipe it with my sleeve. I took a firm hold of the handle, quiet and desperate, leaned against the door and nearly fell into the lobby. It hadn't been locked.

I stood in pitch darkness, but this had a smell of people. There was some kind of animal skin under my feet and somewhere I could hear a clock. I tried to breathe light, pushing the door gently to without closing it. Never burn your bridges, you look stupid when you're drowning. I let the torch beam flick round the lobby walls. The stag's head shook me, watching me with evil marbles. There was a door to the left on the street side which I guessed lead to the sitting-room unless Largo lived upside-down in more ways than one. As soft as I could I took the handle and leaned on the door watching the room inch by

66

inch. No bullet. I could pick out the shape of the furniture.

First things first. I got behind the curtain and opened the bay wide to the street. I nearly choked. The jump didn't bear thinking about so I shut the picture out. The torch-beam splashed from the blanket on the wall to the guitar in the corner, from the reed mats to the sideboard, from the chrome-and-hide chairs to the telephone on the table. This boy had a sense of humour as well. His 'phone number was 0007 but maybe he hadn't thought it out. The sideboard first, starting with the bottom drawer. Old cutlery, beads and a few bits of cheap jewellery. Oil paints and brushes. Paint a hit-man by numbers. They must have belonged to the bird. Second drawer. Old papers, letters, newspaper clippings, bills. I ruffled through noting names, trying to spot a lead, anything. There was a letter from Trinidad that went on about a Black Power group, was Jesus interested? I'd have said the only power that turned Jesus on was Largo Power. Third drawer. A bull-whip coiled neat and sinister at the bottom, lovingly made with plaited leather strips. Who knows? That wasn't what I was after anyway. Under the coil was a revolver, hard in the torchlight and smelling of new oil. Top drawer. A soft-covered file under a pile of tape cassettes. As I pulled it out it spilled clippings. It was fat and worn. Some of the cuttings were loose and some were pasted carefully on thick grey pages, each page dealing with a particular happening. A Kingston paper told a story about a body found in an orchard. Mutilations. The police had no leads. A brawl in a bar where a bloke got his mouth widened by the wrong end of a bottle. A clipping from the *News of the World* about the body of a bird found built into the bedroom cupboard of a house in Birmingham. And so on. There must have been twenty items about blood and gore, all indexed and pasted in. If I sussed it right he must be crazy. Performing was bad enough but to keep a record like a score-card he had to be raving.

The light hit me like a white board and I was already half-way to the window when a bird's voice shouted: 'Who are you?'

Something about her tone stopped me with one foot on the cill. Glancing sideways I could see her shadow on the wall. The shape was enough to stop anybody, but the thing that really brought me up short was the shadow of the gun in her hand. I took my foot off the cill but didn't turn round. 'Lady, you ought to get dressed.'

'Get over by the wall!' I edged next to some kind of voodoo sculpture. 'Now,' the shooter clicked, 'who are you?'

I spoke towards the floor. 'Just a poor old dosser with no place to kip ...'

'Shut up!' The phone tinkled.

'Sweetheart,' I said to the shadow, 'I wouldn't call the fuzz. Think what they might find.' If she saw my face she'd recognize me and it's got to be more difficult to chop a burglar you know. I hoped. I started easing round.

'Keep still!' I felt her moving to my left. 'Look at me. Just your face. Don't move your hands!'

I turned my head slow so she wouldn't mistake fear for fight. In spite of everything some of me was normal enough to appreciate what I saw. She was wearing a wisp of nightie drawn tight over plump black nipples and a pair of tiny panties masking her pubic hair. She looked puzzled and pretty.

'Hey man. Don't I know you?'

I felt stupidly excited. I moved my palms off the wall keeping them in sight, and turned to face her. 'Sure. Anyway, I know you.'

She frowned. 'From the club.' She was pointing the shooter at my crutch. 'What you want?'

I swallowed. 'If you'll ... just point that ... thing another way I'll try and tell you.'

'You tell me now or I blow your balls off!'

I've never thought so quick in my life. 'Well, see, I heard old Jesus keeps more stuff than he needs on the premises. I thought it would be easy to lift. My source got busted and I need the bread.'

She laughed but she wasn't amused. 'Bull *shit*!' She was full of eyes, this girl, crawling all over me. 'You come to spy on Largo. Or ...' she smiled wickedly, 'you come to spy on me.'

I shrugged. 'Believe what you like.'

She stroked her bottom lip with the gun-barrel. 'Yeah. I say you came for me. You know Largo's away. You come for me, sexy bastard.' She threw back her head and laughed. Her boobs swayed under the film of nylon.

'I knew he was away. I didn't come for you.'

She stamped her foot. 'Bad boy! You know what Largo does to fellers who mess with me?'

The conversation was taking a nasty turn. 'Where's Largo?'

She sniffed. 'Liverpool.' She giggled. 'He's back soon. Why you reckon I left the door unlocked, big boy?'

What the bloody hell was I doing nattering to five and a half feet

68

of sex killer at four a.m. anyway? 'Why'd he go to Liverpool? A job?'

She pouted. 'Guess so. He's a fool that man. I told him don't go and now because he's not here he loses a job in London.'

'How's that?'

'I dunno.' The gun snapped up. 'You ask a lotta questions, bad boy.'

'Oh, call me Cain. Mister Cain.' That was probably the most brilliant idea I've ever had. The shooter began to droop.

'Cain. OK.' She grinned. 'You wanna wait for Largo, Mister Cain? He won't be long. He'll tell you all about the job he lost.' She giggled behind her hand.

'No.' I folded my arms. 'I know about Drake.' Her eyes narrowed. 'You know about the job?'

'Sure.'

She frowned. 'You're a devil, you Cain-you. You a friend of Largo? You know a lot, don't you?'

She sat on the arm of the couch and traced circles on the matting with her toe. Her toenails were emerald, her legs were long and golden and her briefs were thin as tape over her hips. She sucked her finger.

'Come on Mister. I know you came for me.' The gun still pointed level. 'You gotta get what you came for, huh?'

I cleared my throat and eyed the window. She saw my glance. 'You know what Largo would do if he found you here? But that's OK. I never tell nothing, you know?' She smiled. 'It's just ... you never know when Largo gets back' She steadied the gun. 'OK Cain. Now you get what you came for.' She stood light and graceful. 'But watch for Largo.'

With one hand she lifted the hem of her nightie clear of her briefs and up over her breasts. They spilled free and quivering. She dropped the nightie on the matting. 'Nice, huh?' I had to agree but in my state I had too many doubts. She stroked the gun-barrel over her belly and down to the dark triangle between her legs. 'Come Mister.' The barrel dug at the top of her panties, easing the nylon down until they stretched in a thin white line across the top of her thighs. Her eyes glittered as she swayed towards me and pressed close, mouth finding mine while one hand pressed the shooter in my ribs. Her free hand groped, unzipped my fly and slipped inside.

The way I saw it she wasn't going to be happy either way and if I stayed Largo was going to make me very unhappy indeed. In one action I grabbed her gun hand with my left and chopped her elbow with my right, using my hip to lever her down. She fell hard, smooth

69

and nude, cussing like a docker. Her left hand had nearly taken the remains of my excitement with it, and I yelped loud. But I had the gun. I threw it hard across the room and leapt for the curtains. The pavement hit me with a wallop that nearly broke my arm but while my legs were in fair shape I wasn't hanging about. I fought clear of the curtaining and felt my hair streaming as I hit the breeze down Cornwall Gardens.

I could hear her cussing from the corner of Gloucester Road.

Twelve

Vista Villas was off Highgate West Hill and the vista in particular was the top end of Hampstead Heath and half the smoke below. It was the sixteenth. I was shagged after two nights on the trot but since the sixteenth has a habit of turning up the day before the seventeenth I had to chance getting nicked by this Carson while I scanned the layout. The way I figured, Carson hadn't met Cain but whatever he was expecting Drake would have told him something and Carson would be double-shocked to see a shiny spade on the doormat come pay-day.

It was a Y-shaped block four storeys high with the lift and stairs wedged in the fork. It sat in its own grounds with no sign of the usual action you get round flats, no screaming mums, no chalk-marks and no bikes left on the flowers. The only sound as I doddled through the gardens in the sun was bird-song, and not much of that. The flats must've been too small or too costly for families. It was the sort of place loved by retired bank-managers and young marrieds with more gelt than sense. They'd had one of those electronic doors set in the entrance, the type that open like Sesame when you step on the mat. The foyer was dark and not rich-looking, being plain walls painted mushroom and a worn carpet on the floor. The letter-boxes lined one wall like luggage-lockers with name-plates. Number 23 was the only box without a name, and the flat itself was on the second floor. After the foyer the light in the stairwell hurt my eyes, sun streaming through a glass wall on each half-landing. There was a lift set back from the stairs but I let it alone because given a choice most folk will use a lift and I wasn't keen to be spotted.

71

I needn't have bothered. During the climb I met no one and didn't hear the lift work. The stairs were easy going, made of marble covered with a strip of blue faded carpet down the middle which spread on the landings a foot short of the walls. Each landing had two doors near the lift. One was the rubbish chute, ugly and sealed with a cast-iron lid, and the other was a cleaner's cupboard smelling of polish and wet rags. A pair of double doors led to the corridors at each floor, three corridors with two flats a side leading off the fork. Because the corridors were internal there was no sunlight, the whole length depending on light from two fittings hard against the ceiling. Number 23 was the last door on the left, second floor. On the nearest half-landing I opened a pane in the glass wall. It was a long way down from the second floor and the garden round the bottom of the staircase was badly kept but there were a couple of tough-looking pipes. The glass wall was fitted with obscure glass so you couldn't enjoy the vista unless you were a tenant tucked up in your gaff, but the effect was like a luminous screen at the back of the stair, a wall of light forcing you to turn your back. I climbed to the top floor. Peering over the balustrade and shading my eyes I could see about half the landing below. The most private spot was in the corner where the handrail met the wall.

I left quietly, walked down the hill to where I'd parked the Mini and drove to Fulham. I spent an hour clearing up, sorted out a suitcase and packed a few bits of clothes. Then I had a word with Marge, telling her I was off on holiday for a fortnight and paid her to the end of the month. She took the money, wished me well and shut the door. Nothing surprised Marge.

Alfred Mehrstein lives in a Peabody Building off the Clerkenwell Road up fifty flights of open stairs without a lift and when his time comes the Lord will pull the trigger as Alfred mounts the thirty-ninth step after a hard day in the Eiger and nobody will know or care. I'm forty years younger than him but by the time I'd reached his landing I hadn't strength enough to knock on his door. It took him several minutes to hide whatever he'd been doing but eventually the door opened on a chain and a pair of specs peered sideways through the crack.

'Harry.' He unlocked. 'Come in. Please.'

He let me through a corridor layered with the dust of his life into an airless sitting-room cluttered with books and photographs. The curtains were drawn against the sun and I had bother unearthing a

72

chair. I picked up a photograph in a silver frame. A very youthful Alfred in a top hat grinned at the camera, a doe-like little mystery on his arm.

'Your wedding?'

He didn't turn. 'Yes.' He was peering into the sideboard. 'The first.' He pulled out a bottle of something amber with a couple of tumblers which he wiped with his handkerchief, lifting his specs to his forehead and holding the glasses up to the crack in the curtains. He poured a drop, passed it to me and dropped his bones into the couch. 'Prosit.' He lowered his specs. They glinted, hiding his eyes.

'Cheerio.' I smacked my lips.

'So?' Said Alfred. 'You are on business?'

'Sort of.' I swirled the cognac round the glass. 'A special bit of business.'

'Ah?' Alfred's professional interest was showing. 'One hundred pounds special?'

I shook my head. 'I want you to do a passport and a few papers. For me.'

There was a long silence while he fumbled with a tin at his elbow and rolled a fag. As I scanned him I realized it was the first time I'd seen him without a hat. His hair was so fine and white you could see his scalp through it. He pushed a fag under his moustache. 'That is very special.' I found a box of matches and lit his fag for him. 'Very special.'

'Will you do it?'

He nodded, squinting through the smoke. 'I will.'

'How much?'

'What exactly do you wish?'

I stood up. 'A passport. Then a few papers – letters, maybe a driving licence, all in a third name.'

He looked interested. 'Not the same name as on the passport?'

I nodded. 'Right.'

He unhooked his specs and started to polish them.

'For you ... fifty pounds for the passport. Twenty for the rest.'

'I wouldn't dream of robbing you. How long?'

Alfred peered at the nicotine stains on the ceiling.

'Three days?'

'Too long.'

He muttered. 'When?'

'Tomorrow night.'

73

'Impossible.'

'Does a hundred quid make it possible?'

He rubbed his eyes. 'For you I must interrupt my work.'

'I know.'

He puffed a cloud of smoke. 'OK.'

'Thanks.'

He finished his cognac and levered himself out of the couch like he was afraid of forgetting a leg.

'Come. Photographs.'

I followed him into a room off the kitchen, picking a path through pots of old cabbage and gummy frying-pans. The room was tiny, lit only by a small window, but when Alfred flicked a switch the place was soaked in white light. The temperature climbed as I stood there. 'How can you stand it?'

He blinked. 'What?'

'Nothing.'

One wall was draped with grey velvet and the space under the window held a drawing-board littered with pencils, pens, inks, rubbers and bits of paper. The shelves on the other two walls were stacked with paper, blue passport books, credit cards and blank driving licences alongside letter-heads of all shapes and sizes, some genuine and some invented. An enlarger crouched over the table next to the board. Alfred cleared a chair and pushed it against the curtain. 'Sit please.' I perched while he rummaged in a drawer and waved a 35 mm Leica which must've set him back a couple of ton. He pulled at the Anglepoise on the wall then shot off five or six frames full-face. 'Good.' He unwound the spool and set the cartridge down on the board. 'Now. The passport. What name please?'

'Charles Armstrong.'

'Middle names?'

'Paul.'

'Born?'

'Bury St Edmunds. Age thirty-three, eyes brown, hair blond, scars left thumb and centre forehead.'

He jotted. 'OK. Next?'

'David Fraser. How about a letter from an insurance company asking for confirmation of date and place of birth. Make it Lincoln.'

He nodded. 'And a letter from your father in . . .'

'Grimsby.' I slipped off the chair. 'Fine.' I followed him into the sitting-room. 'I'll call you tomorrow.' I pulled out a wad and counted off

74

a hundred. 'Take care of that.'

He put an arm round my shoulder like a father as I made for the door. 'Harry ... you are not in trouble?'

I laughed. 'No way, Grandad.'

'What is it?'

'What's what?'

He shook his head as he opened the door. 'Excuse me. I should know better.'

I hadn't meant to say anything. 'You heard of a man called Cain?'

Alfred stiffened, one hand on the door-knob. 'Why are you asking?'

'Have you?'

'Harry ...'

'Forget it.' I jabbed a finger into his chest. 'See you tomorrow. Otherwise *you'll* be in trouble.'

I tried to grin goodbye.

The Hotel Empresa is one of those crawling places that doesn't deserve the name and makes a living out of letting rooms to whores in the afternoons. Since it's just down the street from King's Cross it's handy for three-legged marks hitting town with heavy pockets. But it suited me. The bloke behind the counter didn't look up when I carried in my suitcase, which was just as well or he'd have recognized the expression on my face. The place stank of stale grub and tobacco and you could count the bugs up the walls. The desk-clerk pushed the guest book across without lifting his eyes off the centre-spread crumpet in the *Sun*, which on this occasion went by the name of Lola. I signed David Fraser and he dropped a key on the counter.

'Eight pounds.' He fumbled like a blind man and tucked it in his back pocket.

'Where's my receipt, then, Lola?'

He showed me the whites of his eyes and I could tell this was going to be one of those friendships you remember all your life. His hair was spiky and he wore a sleeveless pullover the same shade of grey as his face. He slammed a book down in a dust cloud and wrote long and hard, copying the signature I'd written in the guest book. I slipped the receipt into my wallet and he turned back to the *Sun*.

'Sixteen. Second floor first door left. Toilet's down the passage.'

The stairs creaked all the way. Room sixteen was what I'd expected. A double bed took up most of the room, pushed hard against the wall next to the door leaving two feet of clear space. There was a sort of wardrobe facing the foot of the bed but no washbasin. I dropped my case on the bed and unpacked quick, hanging a suit on the single wire hanger in the wardrobe. I left the room, locked the door and dropped the key in my pocket.

Lola had gone so I dragged the phone across the counter and dialled Largo's number. It was six o'clock and he'd had time to get back and get mad. I stretched my handkerchief over the mouthpiece.

'Hullo?' Kara's voice.

'Let me speak to Largo.'

'Who's this?'

'Tell him I'm an acquaintance.'

'You got a name, Mister Acquaintance?'

'Never mind. I've got a message for him.'

'Fuck off.' The phone went dead. I sighed. This was not as easy as they made out in the movies. I dialled again.

'Yeah?' Kara.

'I just want a word with Largo ...'

'Go to hell.' She hung up.

I could feel my shirt sticking to my back. A fly buzzed round my head as I tried once more.

'What?' Largo.

'Listen – '

'Who is this, man?'

'It doesn't matter. I want to tell you something about Drake.'

There was a pause. 'So talk.'

I swallowed. 'Drake double-crossed you. He was told to give the contract to you but he sold it to a man called Cain. Got that? Cain.'

'Hey friend – '

'Wait. Cain has arranged to meet Drake's client tomorrow at four o'clock at 23 Vista Villas. Number 23. It's worth a lotta bread, Largo. You know that.'

His voice was tight. 'So what's in this for you, man?'

'Satisfaction.' He began to interrupt. 'And a cut of that fifteen grand. You know where to find Drake? Mason and Coburn, Camden High Street. I'll call you again.' I closed my eyes. 'And Largo ... hear me. Ask Kara about Cain.' I set the phone down, mopping my face. If I sussed right neither Sergeant Drake nor Mister Cain would be causing me much more bother.

Lola came back carrying a ledger. 'That'll be ten pee'.

Thirteen

I got to Vista Villas at two-thirty, walking confident through the gardens like I was visiting, keeping the pose going through the foyer and up the stairs to the top floor. I saw no one but by the time I reached the top my heart was knocking to be let out through my teeth and it wasn't just the exercise. I felt sick. What risk was worth fifteen grand anyway? I straightened my shoulders. Fifteen grand was Freedom. What did a little mutilation mean compared to that?

I heard the lift click and move a couple or three times while I waited and each time found myself stretched like a bow-string. The lift never came as far as the top floor but it did once stop at the floor below, Carson's floor, and shading my eyes as I strained at the balustrade I glimpsed a woman in a print dress pushing through the doors. By two-thirty my hands were so wet I was holding a handkerchief between them and I still reckon that if the lift hadn't signalled then and there I would've cracked and dropped the whole idea. I stationed myself in the corner, hand shielding my eyes from the light on the half-landing. The lift stopped on the floor below and opened its doors. I spent the next ten seconds trying to take in air anywhere except my mouth. The doors started to close and I was relaxing just as a hand forced them apart. Largo stepped out with the air of a bloke with an eye in every pore. He stood as the doors shut behind him, both hands in his jacket pockets, deadpan behind those blind sunglasses. Then he glided across the landing and stood against the wall facing the lift.

He was well turned out in an expensive fawn suit and a rust-coloured shirt, probably silk, with lace foaming round the cuffs. His tie was white, matched by a silk handkerchief in his breast pocket, and his scalp gleamed. He unhooked his shades while I watched and polished them on the white handkerchief, washed-out eyes turned away from the light. I stepped back, scared of those eyes, so that I saw only his feet. He wore hand-made shoes, the left toe tapping to some rhythm he played in his head. I was keeping my own movements slow and considered. A bead of sweat broke on my forehead, trembled, and tumbled down my cheek. I collected it on a forefinger, watched it dangle and drip to the floor. This appointment was turning into a barrel of laughs.

It was dead on four when the lift whined. Largo's foot withdrew fast as a snake and I inched back to the balustrade. He stood against the wall, one hand in his jacket pocket, the other spread against the plaster. He was bent at the waist like a swimmer waiting for the gun. Whoever came through those doors would get it and there was nothing Largo could do to stop himself.

The lift had arrived but the doors weren't opening – they were stuck, surely. A crack. Widening. Like Largo before him the man in the lift had stood well back facing the doors. Largo moved so fast he was hard to follow. He seemed to stretch from the wall to the lift in a flicker, legs following like the shot in a catapult, head and arms stabbing into the car. For a second he was seen only from the hips down, one knee bent, toe poised on the marble like a sprinter snapped on the instant of go. And in that pose he began to slide back like a statue on a pedestal. The fawn jacket emerged hem-first, the snappy cut sloping into sight an inch at a time. His head, black and dome-like, was set down in his shoulders facing up towards the man in the lift. The stranger was tall, blond public-school hair even now in place. His features were even and impassive as an umpire's at a cricket match and his hands were clamped round Largo's wrists at shoulder height, holding them apart like the wings of a chicken on the table. And between Largo's hands a glint of wire, now invisible, then flashing like an electric arc. The edge of the carpet snapped back into place under Largo's feet as he slid slow and regular backwards until his left heel touched the wall. The stranger was straightening Largo's back, little by little sapping the strength from his spine. They faced each other, eyes level, Largo's shades reflecting the calm grey of the other's. The stranger was forcing Largo's fists inch by inch up and towards each other like preparing for handcuffs. The wire sparked, slackened,

78

and dangled mid-way to Largo's chest and still the stranger pressed on. Largo was fixed flat to the wall, forearms crossed before his face and hands above his head. Like a dancer the stranger raised his right knee, selecting the spot in Largo's crutch before leaning his weight with the care of a doctor finding where it hurt. Largo grunted. It was the first sound made since the lift had opened.

The stranger had Largo's arms crossed above his head and pinned to the wall, wire dangling in a pretty loop under his chin. Largo's hands began to slide down and apart, tracing an arc over his shoulders into a pose for crucifixion. The stranger's knee snuggled into Largo's groin while the wire started to mark a line across his throat. The veins in Largo's neck and temples bulged and his teeth parted over a wad of tongue. He coughed. His fingers released the wooden grip at each end of the wire into the palms of the stranger. Largo's shades fell to the floor, showing eyes like washed-out plums. He made a sound and his foot jerked an inch off the marble. The stranger held him.

A movement. The stranger lowered his knee until he stood feet apart braced against Largo's hands. He straightened and stepped back. Largo posed like a saint, arms outstretched and feet together till he began to slide sideways down the wall dragging his left hand, to fall along the marble border. His face was turned upwards, opaque plums bulging at me.

I watched the back of the stranger's head, lank blond hair fringing his collar as he bent over the corpse. He showed no sign of exertion, hands hanging loose by his sides and the slope of his shoulders normal like he'd just shook hands. There was no mistaking Cain. Then, as if somebody had tapped his shoulder, he turned his head and I found myself looking into the untroubled eyes of a man about to introduce himself. He stepped backwards over the corpse, eyes on mine, and mounted the stairs.

And I just stood. If this was the moment it wasn't like I'd imagined it, this helplessness. Harry Grant crouched like a rabbit in the headlights waiting for Mister Death. Death's form wavered as he stood on the half-landing silhouetted against the wall of light, vague as a shadow. In the same instant, like a clap of thunder, the lift whined into action. The silhouette tensed, listening, then receded. 'Tell your friend Carson . . .' the words were so soft I hardly heard them '. . . treachery warrants reprisal.' I felt a sound begin in my throat, I don't know what, but before my tongue could collect it Death had gone. I was blinking at the sunlight.

The lift doors opened like a bank vault in the silence and a bloke stepped out. He was elderly, carried a cane, and wore a carnation in his button-hole. He glanced at me but didn't pause on his way through the doors. The lift shut and I stood staring at the wall. I took the stairs one at a time. Largo lay where Cain had left him and I tried to stay out of range of those eyes. A moment's panic. Me, a hit-man? I must be crazy. Then my fingers started to warm and I could feel colour flooding my cheeks. Fifteen grand.

First to deal with the late and unlamented Largo. He'd gone down in a nasty way but that had no bearing on the practical side of his disposal. My brain was getting back into gear after storage in the deep-freeze. I opened the cleaner's cupboard. It wasn't a palace but it would do. Avoiding the sight of the wire bedded in Largo's throat I gripped his lapels, unhooked his arm from the balustrade and dragged him across the floor. I squeezed a broom and a tin of polish against the back wall and set about packing Largo tidy as possible. It was difficult because his legs wouldn't stay where they were put but I got the door closed eventually.

I combed my hair and straightened my tie. This was what it was all about. I pushed through the doors and stood outside number 23. If I'd been a religious man I'd have offered a prayer. As it was I took a deep breath, cleared my throat and knocked quietly on the door.

A thin man stood on the threshold, all bones and cheeks so high his eyes slanted, crisp black hair and ears that stood out from his head. Behind him I could see a short squat figure, hands in pockets and specs glinting in the light from the door.

'Mr Carson?'

The thin man shook his head and beckoned me in. 'Wait.' He slipped through a door down the passage while the short feller leaned against the wall breathing heavily round a wad of chewing-gum, watching. The hall needed a coat of paint and had no furniture except a telephone on a coil of flex on the floor. There wasn't even a light bulb. The thin man poked his head out. 'Come.' I pushed past the bloke in the passage towards the door, feeling his eyes on the back of my neck. It was a small nearly empty room with two windows on one wall both open to the heath. There was no carpet and the dust on the floor showed the tracks of the only furniture there – two cheap armchairs and a small table holding a bottle of whisky and a few glasses. A man had risen from the armchair in the corner, leaving a book face-down on the arm and a briefcase on the floor. He was dressed in a three-piece charcoal pin-stripe suit and a white shirt with one of those detachable collars you seldom see nowadays. He held himself erect, watch-chain looped across a stomach flat as a board, shoulders back and chin up. His moustache was trimmed to perfect proportions, not a hair out of place. I reckoned he was aged about fifty. He plucked his watch from his waistcoat pocket and flicked open the lid with his thumbnail, glanced at it, snapped it shut and dropped it back as he stepped forward. His eyes were friendly and he held out his hand, half-smiling, eyebrows raised.

I took his hand. 'Mr Carson? My name is Cain.'

Fourteen

'Permit me to offer you a drink. I have only whisky, I'm afraid.' Carson spoke with a port-and-Tory voice drenched with generations of privilege and what the upper classes call Breeding. I mean he must've had me figured the moment I opened my mouth but then he wasn't hiring me for elocution lessons.

'Thank you.'

He splashed some whisky into a tumbler and handed it over as the thin bloke returned and shut the door. He didn't say much, the thin man, just stood with his back to the door, arms folded. Carson was looking puzzled. 'Where is Mr Drake? He was supposed to be with you, was he not?'

'He wasn't there.'

Carson scanned his watch again. 'I dare say he will arrive in a few minutes. Let's not allow his absence to delay our discussion.' He sat down and crossed his legs, arranging the creases in his trousers. 'Sit down please, Mr Cain.' He placed the tips of his fingers together 'Your selection has been a process of some deliberation, as I imagine you have guessed. Surprisingly difficult.'

'I don't advertise.'

His smile was hardly there. 'Naturally.' He sipped at his whisky. 'Yours is a talent which . . . regrettably, must remain unsung.' He didn't belong in that bleak room in his starched collar. 'However, if his reports are to be believed the excellent Mr Drake has performed his function as required, and, subject to my satisfaction, will have earned his not inconsiderable fee.' He sipped again. 'Your . . . colleagues are difficult to assess, Mr Cain, for the same reasons that they are difficult to contact. A man in my position is, after all, so very vulnerable, a prey to every confidence trickster, charlatan and sadist willing to take the risk.' He raised his glass to well-moulded lips. 'Our researches, or rather the man Drake's researches, exposed an interesting sprinkling of aberrations. There was for instance a candidate who appeared to claim responsibility for the assassination of the late President Kennedy. The curious fact is that our man Drake was actually giving this candidate serious consideration until then.'

I nodded. 'You can't be too careful.' The breeze from the heath rolled balls of dust across the parquet floor. Carson stroked his moustache with four perfect fingernails. 'In a sense the proof of your profession rests in your inability to furnish either credentials or proof. In the final analysis my decision must rest upon a judgement of character.'

I hoped I looked amused. 'So you tested my character?'

Carson raised his eyebrows. 'Not I, Mr Cain. Not yet.'

I wasn't smiling now. 'So of course the performance on the stairs was nothing to do with you?'

'The stairs?'

I drank. 'You'll find your friend in the cupboard.'

Carson's glass was arrested half-way to his mouth. He set it on the floor and nodded at the thin man who left the room. 'I will not pretend to understand your insinuations. Mr Logan or Mr Craig outside will confirm your explanation, if you have one, when they return.'

I scanned him evenly. 'I don't mind, Carson, get that straight. You set the test and you take the consequences.'

Carson allowed an edge of irritation into his voice. 'Mr Cain. If you wish to make an observation please do so as clearly as possible.'

Logan came in and reached Carson in two strides.

'I have,' I said.

Logan whispered into Carson's ear. Carson didn't move, eyes clamped on mine while he listened. Then he nodded and Logan left. Carson cleared his throat. 'We now appreciate the reasons for your confusion. The man you met on the stairs had nothing to do with us or the organization we represent.' He drank. 'Like you I cannot furnish proof. I ask you to accept my word.'

I spoke through my teeth. 'Great. Carson, I warn you the only proof I need from you is the money.'

He nodded. 'Logan tells me that the ... man on the landing was a ... Negro?' He carried the bottle to me and splashed a couple of fingers into my glass. 'That eases my mind. One of the unsuccessful

83

candidates interviewed by Mr Drake was, I believe, a Negro. Drake advised against his selection because he doubted the man's sanity.'

He sat down. 'No doubt you will understand that I sought a man who did not enjoy the prospect for its own sake.' He sighed. 'From Mr Drake's description I gathered that the Negro was ... rather enamoured of his work.' He examined his fingernails. 'Mr Drake suspected that the Negro may have borne his disappointment at rejection too heavily. You, Mr Cain, I fear, bore the brunt of that disappointment.' He sounded sorry but satisfaction shone out of his face like sunshine in Spain.

There was a thump from the hall and the sound of something getting dragged across the floor. Poor old Jesus. He lived for thirty years to find his only purpose in death. Carson rose and looked into the hall. 'An unpleasant method.' He was pale when he sat down.

'Unpleasant, but his,' I told him.

He leaned forward on his elbows. 'Your reaction was justified and the ultimate responsibility must rest, as you suggested, with me. I ask you to regard the matter closed.'

'I had.'

Carson frowned at the dial of his pocket-watch. 'Time is precious. It seems we shall have to reconcile ourselves to the absence of our friend Drake.' He rested both hands on the arms of his chair. 'Now. The purpose which brings you here. Unlike you I am not a Londoner. I am not English.' You could've fooled me. 'I say that with pride because my countrymen, saddened by recent experience, have come to regard themselves as the last bulwark of all that is meaningful in the British tradition.' He drew himself up.

'I am an Ulsterman, Mr Cain, one of many to whom the description British is not a meaningless concept, nor an outmoded word to be ridiculed in some cellar peopled by denims and beards.' So Carson was just another Mick in a Tory suit marching at the front of the column. 'Clearly you are not politically motivated, and that is a situation desired by my organization. You are a professional, ready to fulfil certain obligations in return for an agreed remuneration and I imagine that you prefer not to regard your subject as a personality or a political symbol. However, it is necessary that you listen even though privately you may not accept my argument.' He took a deep swallow at the glass and seemed lost in thought for several seconds.

'Northern Ireland is British, Mr Cain, has been British for some centuries and shall ever remain so. Yet there are those who seek to

84

deny that fact and to wrest from us that which we hold most dear. Our pride in our heritage, our Britishness.' Logan returned and took up position against the door. Carson looked up and continued. 'These men would achieve their aims in a variety of ways, by trickery, deception, twisted legislation, by the bomb and by the gun. Trickery may be exposed, deception revealed and deviant legislation unravelled.' His voice had raised. 'But fire must be fought with fire.' He smiled, a great ear-to-ear snap and I thought, Christ, he's mad. 'And that is your purpose. Imagine that your role, however slight, is one lick of flame in the furnace which will eventually consume Republicanism and its every espouser.' He gestured. 'But of course motivation is not your concern.'

It was warm in the room in spite of the breeze. I walked to the windows and stared out at the heath. A man, an ordinary bloke in check shirt and grey flannels was walking his dog across the grass not far from the building. His dog ran ahead, spun into a crouch, then lolloped back, great muddy paws all over the bloke's flannels. It was crazy. Out there a feller was taking his collie on a ramble and in here was a maniac screaming about a cause worth less than a fart in this day and age. I mean first and foremost I'm Harry Grant and I'm not perfect but if I needed a national label to tell me who I am I'd go out and jump under a fourteen bus. Carson wasn't a man, he was an idea in a pin-stripe suit, an idea that Harold pulled out with his eye in 1066. I turned to face him.

'Fine. Who's the mark?'

'I beg your pardon?'

'Who's the mark?' I spread my hands. 'The subject.'

'Ah. Sit down please.' I sat. 'The Irish Republican Army ...' I could see he had bother with the words, 'the Irish Republican Army is an organization with multitudinous connections. You are obviously aware that they are active and strong here in England. Visits by activists to London are a common-or-garden occurrence – after all one does not need a passport to travel between provinces. Naturally one draws attention to the foolishness of allowing similar concessions to the populace of Eire, but only time will ensure that Westminster perceives the folly of that policy.' He bit on his anger and continued. 'London in particular closets one known cell, possibly more. Now. My organisation has recently acquired information which leads us to believe that a meeting is about to be held in London. We understand the purpose is twofold.' He covered the distance to the window in three exact strides.

'Firstly to discuss and streamline the command structure of the IRA in England. Secondly to conduct the trial of a turncoat. The IRA has its own methods of dealing with traitors.' He turned his back to the light and leaned on the window cill. 'A very important man, a senior officer of the Belfast Command, is scheduled to attend the meeting. His visit will last one week, commencing on the nineteenth.' He left the window and loomed over my chair. 'His name is Frisby, and his loss would cause inestimable damage to the IRA.' He folded his arms and stared into my face. 'Find that man. Rid my countrymen of one more cancer and you earn their undying gratitude.'

I watched him. 'Fine. Provide the information and the job gets done. But like you said I don't concern myself with politics and gratitude doesn't buy boots for the baby. Where's the money?'

Carson raised his eyes and signalled to Logan. He gave me the willies, Logan, because he never said a word and his feet didn't seem to touch the ground when he walked. He left the room and came back carrying the kind of suitcase that sells for a couple of quid in Marks and Spencer. It looked heavy and he placed it carefully at my feet. Carson tapped it with a polished toe. 'Ten thousand pounds. The advance.' Good for Mister Cain, he certainly knew his value. I rested the case on my knees and flipped the latches. It was all there in used tens and fives. I checked the bundles for paper sandwiches but I needn't have bothered. My hands were sweating and I dared not catch Carson's eye. It was like heaven had opened and all the angels had let go with one great hallelujah. 'And ten thousand to follow. On completion,' Carson was saying. 'As to the details ...' he pulled a folder from his briefcase and laid it on the money. 'This dossier will furnish all the information you will require ... names, dates, and a personal history of the subject. You have two days to familiarize yourself with the contents, following which you have, as I said, one week to completion. When you wish to contact me, place an advertisement in the personal column of *The Times* including a precise time and a telephone number. Your advertisement should be headed Boyne.' His eyes flickered. 'I shall of course expect more than your word.'

I snapped the latches shut. 'Tell me. Why don't you people handle this yourselves? Why pay for it?'

His lips stretched over well-kept teeth. 'You will surely understand that my organization cannot afford to be linked to this act.' Since the only link between him and the fading of friend Frisby was Harry Grant it was obviously time to end the conversation before he started going into detail. I picked up the case and followed him to the door. The three of them pressed close on me in the hall, the squat Craig making no effort to move as I passed him. Carson held out a hand. 'I should add...' I'd been expecting it for the last hour, 'that if you fail ... my organization does not recognize failure, just as you do not recognize causes. If you fail, please be assured that no corner on earth will protect you against our brand of retribution.' He smiled, charmingly. 'Good luck, Mister Cain.' The door closed quietly behind me.

Fifteen

It might've been the heft of the loot in my hand or the choir in my head, I don't know, but either way I wasn't smart enough when I stepped into the street. A car engine started. A black Citroën DS waited twenty yards up the hill. It had to be him. Suddenly I was clawing the suitcase to my chest with both hands, and if Cain hadn't known what was in the case he'd certainly sussed now because Killer Grant had told him the story in one move. I lowered the case and tried to think. Carson or me. If Cain chose me now he'd get the bread but lose Carson and his lads. And he wanted Carson bad – hadn't Carson just tried to set him up? Hadn't he just hired someone else? Carson would lead him to me in the end anyway – that is if Cain didn't hit him too soon. I walked jerkily down the hill to the Mini, fumbling at the lock. I chucked the case on the front seat, climbed in and sat trying to steady my hands while I watched the Citroën in the mirror. There was nothing to lose. I started the car and let her roll slowly down Highgate West Hill. The Citroën shrank into the background. As I rounded the bend near the shops I put my foot down. Cain had made his choice and H. Grant had just borrowed time. How long? I was shuddering as I headed for King's Cross.

Ten grand spread on the stains of the hotel eiderdown was a sight conducive to a drop of old-fashioned rapture and although this particular bed must've been accustomed to the kiss of cash it certainly hadn't seen such rapture since Leeds won the cup. The bundles covered the surface laid out like draughts, tens alternating with fives, and I scanned them from every angle the room allowed. I sat down, stood up and trickled them over my head like cornflakes, fighting the bubbles of laughter that grew in my belly and popped in my mouth like song.

After an hour or so I collected control and packed the money back in the case. I took it with me to the bathroom down the corridor and kept one eye on it while I washed. It wasn't a healthy bathroom but I was in no state to worry about contagious diseases with ten grand crushing the bubbles in the lino. Back in the room I circled it while I dressed and finished up with a shirt like a strait-jacket. About six I carried it out past the desk in reception.

'Going?' Lola glanced up from his paperback.

'Staying.' I skipped down the steps and dodged the traffic across Euston Road to King's Cross. There is a row of phones in the extension to the station but like the rest of British Rail two out of three are on strike. Eventually I wedged me and the case into a booth, spread my coppers out on the shelf and dialled Alfred's number. 'Alfred? Got my things?'

'They are almost ready, Harry.'

'Right. Bring them to the Hotel Empresa about half-seven.'

'Yes. Where is that?'

'You know the road opposite ...' A man was buying a paper at the stall across the arcade. Crowds rolled across the rubber between him and me and I lost him several times in the mass. A thin man. Logan. He looked towards me and the mob closed, gaped, and he was gone.

'Harry?' I scanned the bookstall. Two women were buying magazines. 'Harry?'

The receiver was slippery. 'Yeah?'

A pause. 'Are you in trouble?'

I touched the case with my foot. 'No.'

Alfred coughed. 'You were talking about the Hotel Empresa.'

I told him where it was. 'Alfred, listen. Hang about King's Cross first, OK? Grab a brass and bring her to the hotel.'

'You want a girl, Harry?'

'No. Book a double room. I'll give you the money.'

Alfred's voice raised. 'A girl? For me? And why should I want a prostitute?'

'Belt up and do as I say,' I shouted. 'Look ... put your shoes outside the door so I'll know where you are.'

He sounded old and quiet. 'I hope you know what you are doing.'

'None better.' I hung up. The walls of the booth were bothering me

89

and I was not feeling well. A baggy-eyed blonde came and stood outside the booth tapping her foot. I looked her dead in the eye with my hand on the receiver. She turned away sharp when I picked it up and started to dial again. Crab was having one of his off-days and didn't fancy driving. It took five quid to buy off his mood. He sounded pissed. I couldn't see Logan on the way back to the Empresa but I could almost feel his breath on my neck.

I hung my jacket in the wardrobe, unlocked Carson's suitcase and chucked the money into a pile at the foot of the bed. Carson's case and mine were about the same size only mine was cheaper. I stuffed seven hundred in various pockets and opened my own case wide on the pillow. It took a while to pack the notes so my case didn't look bulky and almost as long again to get the lid locked. The key I put in my wallet. I checked the room, then pushed a pillow into Carson's case. It wasn't enough so I scooped up the bedside mat and bundled it on top, coughing in the puff of dust as I forced the lid shut. I forced that key down a crack in the skirting and pushed the case under the bed. Then I took off my watch, lay on the bedspread with my feet on my case and shut my eyes.

I woke with a bounce, reaching for the money at my feet. The room was getting dim. I stood up and switched on the light, yawning and feeling like a playground for bed-bugs. Case in hand, I slipped into the corridor. Alfred's room wasn't hard to find because nobody else was crazy enough to put their shoes outside the door in a cat-house like that.

Alfred sat stiff as a bolt on a chair against the far wall wearing his hat and coat but no shoes. His cheeks were flushed and I've never seen a bloke so relieved. He gripped my hands. 'Harry! Where have you been?' The cause of all this bother sat on the bed. She couldn't have been a day over fourteen and looked scared to death in her scarlet mini-skirt. There were holes in her tights and I reckoned she'd bought her stilettos secondhand off Minnie Mouse. Her mouth was larded crimson and she was sending semaphore with her eyelashes. Her knees gripped a yellow plastic handbag.

'You dirty old man.' I dropped the case. 'I didn't know you fancied the kiddie-winkies.'

Alfred covered his eyes. 'Such a time I have had. Terrible. She was all I could find and then you don't come . . .' he shuddered.

The kid felt safer with the both of us. 'All he wants to do is look,' she waved her lashes at Alfred. 'You get blokes like him you know.'

'I know. But do you?'

'Anyway,' she pouted, 'I don't care. Costs the same, three quid. Bet he won't pay.'

I peeled off a five. 'I'm his uncle.'

She grabbed the note, puffed with pride. 'What about you, lovie?' Her clammy little fingers trickled down my cheek. 'Want to wet your winkle?'

I patted her hand. 'Ta, no. Any other time would've been perfect but tonight me and my nephew have got to talk business.'

'Well, I'm at the station when you fancy it.' She lurched to the door, tiny bum twitching. 'See you, Pretty Boy.' She made a face at Alfred.

Alfred was shaking. 'Lieber Gott.' He sat down. 'The things I must do for my friends.'

'Your friends appreciate it.' I sat on the bed. 'What do I owe you?'

He produced a packet. 'Ten pounds for this . . . terrible room.' His face wrinkled like old newspaper.

I counted out the money. 'There you go.' I opened the packet. 'Thanks a lot.'

He sighed. 'You will not tell me what this is about?'

I shook my head. 'There's one last thing I'd like you to do.'

He raised his hands. 'Not like . . .'

'Not like, no. Listen. See this case? In about an hour a taxi will pick you up on the corner. The driver's a mate of mine. He'll take you home. Leave the case with him, OK?'

Alfred nipped the ends of his moustache. 'That is all?'

'That's all, Grandad.' I patted the case. 'Important. Very important. Look after it.' I held out a hand. 'Cheers. Take care.'

He gripped my hand. 'I will see you again?'

'You know me. I'll be around sometime.'

He was looking dejected when I left the room.

By eight I was waiting on the pavement with Carson's case. Logan was near – I could feel him and I could smell him and I wondered if he knew. At five past a taxi hit the kerb and stopped half up the pavement. Crab fell out, tie undone and jacket hanging loose. His eyes were bloodshot and he stank like a brewery.

'Right.' He swayed. 'Where to?'

I didn't smile. 'Put the case in. Slow as you like.'

His face split into a sloppy grin. 'Harry . . .'

I hissed through my teeth. 'Shut up.'

He froze, arm outstretched, shrugged, picked up the case and walked round the bonnet to the luggage platform where he strapped it down. I climbed in the back, slammed the door and twisted to scan the street through the rear window. Just up the road a pair of headlights blinked on. Crab jumped into the driving seat and opened the partition window, puffing clouds of booze.

'So what's it all about?'

'I'm being watched. Just drive to Victoria station.'

Crab's eyes glittered. 'Right. Let's lose the bastard.'

'No!'

He looked bewildered. 'I thought you said you was being watched?'

'So I bloody am. Just you drive straight and easy. Whatever you do don't lose him.'

He shook his head. 'Bloody stupid.' The taxi jumped the pavement into the centre of the road. A Cortina eased out behind us and followed at four lengths.

I knocked on the window. 'Crab. Listen.' He turned his head and the taxi swung towards a parked car. 'And keep your eyes on the road.' The radio was squawking so he flipped the switch as we joined the traffic in Euston Road. 'When we get to Victoria I'm going to book this case in Left Luggage. I want you to come back to the corner near the hotel and pick up an old boy, a mate of mine called Alfred. He'll be wearing a hat and coat and carrying a case. Take him back to Clerkenwell. He'll leave the case in the cab. Strap it on the platform and don't let it out of your sight.'

'If you say so.' Crab hiccupped and steered the cab down Great Portland Street. 'What's this all about?'

I pulled a seat flap down and sat next to the window. 'The case the old boy will leave is stuffed with junk.'

Crab yelped. 'Christ, Harry. You know I don't like getting involved with drugs.'

'Just this once, is all. You don't have to do anything. Just operate normal for a few days and stay in radio contact. I'll 'phone you when I want you.'

'No.'

I glanced behind. The Cortina was still there. 'Don't be a mug. You're not getting involved in anything.'

'I don't like anything to do with drugs.'

'It's worth a few quid to me.' We spun into Park Lane. 'Did you hear what I said?'

Crab scratched his ear. 'Who's the party behind, then?'

'Oh, nobody special. Anyway he's following me, not you. A sort of watch-dog. He'll stay with me at Victoria after you've gone.'

Crab cussed a bloke on a moped. 'How much d'you reckon it's worth to you?'

I pondered. 'Dunno. The stuff's worth about three hundred. Say twenty quid?'

He tried to scan me in the mirror. 'If it's worth three ton we oughta be thinking bigger than that. I mean, there's the inconvenience. I was going to have a few days off.'

I sighed. 'Twenty-five.'

'Thirty-five.'

'Bollocks. Think I'm a bloody charity?' The taxi skirted the wall to Buck House. 'Thirty.'

Crab grinned in the mirror. 'That's it.'

'Watch the road.'

The Cortina was just behind.

We ploughed into the forecourt through a herd of cabs and pulled up in a chain of jerks outside the entrance. I counted off a few notes, screwed them into a ball and shoved them through the window. Crab opened his hand and gaped. 'Oy. There's near three hundred here.'

'Belt up. One more thing. Book me a single to L.A. for the twenty-fourth.'

'L.A. what?' Crab was suddenly sober.

'Los bloody Angeles. When I call you bring the case and the ticket. And don't get ideas about the change.'

Crab's face was a sort of grey colour. 'Jesus. Look Harry, I don't want no involvement in . . .'

'Trust me.' I opened the door and waited while he unstrapped the case. 'And don't monkey about with that junk, there's a good lad. I swear if I go down you come with me. All right?'

He looked hurt. 'Harry.'

'See you.'

'Take care.'

I carried Carson's caseful of carpet into the booking hall, waiting for Logan to get in range. He wasn't long. Walking under the wrought-iron and glass roof at Victoria is like having a doddle through a forest

93

of pines – not that I've ever been in a pine forest. The benches were scattered with dazed swedes watching a queue leak from platform thirteen while the loud-speakers boomed and twanged. The rush was over and the station looked like a battlefield when they've all limped home. Logan stayed twenty yards away when I got to the Left Luggage counter. I booked Carson's case in and collected my tab. Logan followed me to the caff and waited outside while I drank two cups of British Rail tea.

At nine I joined the queue for the taxis. It didn't matter if he lost me now.

Sixteen

I had a bad night. Sweating sheets didn't help and by the time I started thinking of Carson I'd already seen off the Sandman with fresh-frozen eyeballs and dreams that went bump in the dark. I crawled out of bed at eight like a dosser from a gutter and tried to have a wash in the basin down the passage but there was no soap, no plug and no hot water. My clothes felt diseased and I had bother sorting out a shirt that fitted. At nine I strolled down to the local caff and treated myself to eggs and bacon and wished I hadn't. Two mugs of coffee made it worse. But then you can't go for years with a slice of toast in the morning and expect to bob up chuckling after a plate of grease. I grabbed a late edition of the *Express* somebody had left behind but I didn't seem able to focus on the print so I sat there like a dummy waiting for the sweat to dry on my forehead. I'd got ink from the paper on my fingers and I needed a holiday.

The sun was double bright outside and even the traffic on the Euston Road was louder than usual. People pushed me about on the pavement because I couldn't point my feet straight. I was climbing the steps to the hotel when I spotted the Cortina parked fifty yards up the road and it might have been my nerves or the breakfast but whatever it was I had to grab the railings and wait for the cartwheels in my gut to ease off. I am as a person very cool and not normally given to nervous attacks but that Cortina was starting to get right up my nose. I had to do something eventually, so why not before I ended up twitching in the nut-house? The bloody car sat against the kerb, sleek and fat, the windscreen reflecting hazy blue from the sky, bold as a brass on a bed. The blood knocked at my temples as I ran upstairs and got the keys to the Mini.

I started slow, turning towards the Euston Road and giving him plenty of time to get behind me. I watched him pull out from the kerb and start following at about twenty yards. And I hated him. The traffic on the Euston Road at half-ten is heavy, what with the day's artics starting to trundle into town along with wives from Luton and Hatfield scheming how to spend the old man's bread. We moved slow and sedate in the middle lane, stopping every fifty yards for another traffic light. I was in no hurry. When the cross-traffic was slow getting away I marked time on the green light waiting for the junction to clear rather than carving a gap like I normally did, and I stopped on the amber each time whether there was room or not. We crept down the underpass choking in the fumes and I was ever so courteous, letting the motors from the left filter in ahead of me. The Cortina was three cars behind.

I was first in the queue at Park Square traffic lights and the time had come to find out what my mate was made of. I slipped into first and held the clutch down, easing off the handbrake and feeling the wheel get slippery in my palms.

Amber.

Clutch out accelerator down hard right. The Mini howled across the tarmac on two wheels in an arc for Regent's Park. Hell exploded behind me but I had my eye on the oncoming traffic. I glimpsed the shock on the face of the driver in the outside lane as he stood on the anchors and got shunted by the truck behind. The meat waggon next to him lurched so bad I thought he'd somersault his load. I took Park Square East at fifty, leaning on the horn. A van parked across the lane like the wall of death and the facing traffic was still. I hit the kerb behind the van and carved forty feet of palings alongside the pavement. The Mini bounced three feet off the kerb ahead of the van, hitting the camber at an angle and sliding sideways for ten yards before I could wrestle her straight. I hit the brake and slewed into the Outer Circle just ahead of a Viva, straightened and thundered down the asphalt. As I slowed for Park Square West I saw the Cortina jump the pavement and squeeze between the Viva and a Marina. I crashed into second and took the corner broadside on, zipping down the right-hand side of the road towards the cars strung out across the Euston Road. The horn must've been having an effect because the line broke like elastic and the Mini took the crossing into Park Crescent without touching the downside of the camber. Back into second and a wide sweep into Portland Place. The traffic was like a weld. The Cortina stopped behind with six inches to spare, sunshine sparking off the windscreen like a mirror. I was probably cussing louder than anyone.

We drifted down Portland Place and did a neat U-turn at New Cavendish Street, heading back towards the Euston Road. He stayed with me through the traffic and kept a steady two lengths behind as we picked up speed over the flyover and down the incline towards Westway. I slithered towards the Paddington exit, testing his nerve as we approached the roundabout at the bottom. There are three exits on the roundabout and I put my foot down on the circle, listening to the tyres scream on the way round. I made a couple of false dives and the Cortina echoed every inch like a dog on a lead. I thought he wasn't going to make it as I lurched into the St John's Wood turnoff. That exit takes you up to a circle over the canal and down into a tunnel under the flyover. I hit the tunnel at seventy in a roar that bounced off the walls while the John Citizens to my left honked and flashed their lights. The traffic lights at the top were green and I chucked the Mini left. He was still behind me.

I carried him with me over the rail bridge and left into a white crescent. At the end of the crescent the filter for Westway swoops left, grading up towards the flyover as it passes over Paddington. Westway at this point is wide and fast, closed in by four-foot walls like a channel. I hummed up the incline at fifty in third, grabbing speed and changing into fourth as I lanced into the traffic heading west. It's like flying up there because the walls blinker everything except chimneys and roofs and there's no real sense of place. The Mini was better in a tight situation and I began to think I'd made a mistake hitting the open road. The Cortina was five lengths behind, marking easy time, when a Mercedes ducked from the centre into the space between us. The flyover was curving on a slow bend to the left and by pulling ahead of the Mercedes I got a tanker between me and the Cortina. I got two lengths ahead of the tanker, the Mercedes catching up, then pulled in sharp to the centre lane, braking so the tanker drew close. I could see the driver cussing as he changed down. The Mercedes hissed past. Three seconds behind came the Cortina, travelling fast, one arm shielding the driver's face from the sun as he strained ahead. I ducked into the slow lane behind a coach, nudging close to the chrome.

Two minutes later I passed the Cortina waiting on the hard shoulder. If I hadn't been so close to the coach I'd have seen him before but as it was I was on him before I could figure the next move. He pulled out on my tail. I changed down, swore, checked the mirror and passed the coach windows like Apollo. In a matter of seconds I was tipping eighty in the middle lane, which was not very healthy. Ahead was a Capri looming larger by the second, and on his left an old Mayflower shaking itself to death at a steady thirty. There wasn't much choice. As I glimpsed the three-bar sign for the Shepherd's Bush filter I skipped into the fast lane and the Capri, the Mayflower and I drew level at the same second, fanning out at our different speeds. The one-bar warning flicked past and the painted reservation at the turn-off widened like a knife-blade. I turned left hard as the Mini would take it, checking the fright in the Capri as I skimmed his windscreen knowing that the Mayflower wasn't that far behind. I missed the edge of the dividing wall by inches, straightened twenty feet ahead of the Mayflower and started slackening for the roundabout ahead. The Cortina swayed in after the Mayflower almost sideways, smoke streaming from his tyres, rocked, straightened, slewed again, then grabbed speed in a series of diminishing corrections that forced the Mayflower close to the wall. He was travelling too fast, but maybe he didn't know the road. I hit the roundabout like I was heading straight through and heeled left at the last moment. I swear the wing-mirror scraped the wall. I fought the wheel straight, heard the tyres wail, then the terrible thunder of a ton of steel and chrome ploughing into concrete. The mirror. The Cortina was buckling into a pile of steaming metal against the wall, bits slicing the air like shrapnel down the incline and into the twenty-foot drop below.

I took the half-mile down to Shepherd's Bush quiet and easy giving myself time to calm, negotiating the roundabout like Dad on Sunday morning, then drifted back up the opposite carriageway. Across the gap at the top half-a-dozen motors had slewed to a stop and two men were running towards the roundabout waving down the traffic. Others were running towards the wreck. You couldn't see much through the steam. As I coasted back along Westway three ambulances howled past in the opposite direction.

I found a meter half a block from the hotel and sat quiet for a bit. I felt shagged. The weight of the situation was starting to bend me. Christ, the things some people will do for money. How long before

98

they shoved the bloody gun into my hands? I got out slow and stood stretching on the sidewalk before locking up. I walked back to the hotel staring at the paving. As I reached the steps a hand gripped my arm. 'Cain.' My mind lurched. Logan stood close, fingers biting into my biceps and I stared disbelievingly into eyes hard as the pavement. 'I want to talk to you.' I watched his mouth. 'They found Drake this morning. Listen to me. I know your type and I despise everything you stand for.' His head was set deep into his shoulders like he was cold. 'Whether or not you are directly responsible for Drake's death is immaterial. I know you played your part in it. Now please believe me when I say that from now until you fulfil your obligations I shall be watching you twenty-four hours a day. Whether you see me or not I shall be there.' His fingers tightened. 'And I assure you that you will not lose me as easily as you seem to have lost Mr Craig.' He dropped my arm. 'Remember. I need no excuse. It will give me the greatest pleasure to have you killed where you stand.' He pumped his hands into his pockets and wheeled away.

I stood on the first step. My legs felt weak and I had a headache.

Seventeen

It was the nineteenth and I woke knowing Carson's mark was near. So was Logan. And who else? I lay staring at the stains on the ceiling for ten minutes before my nerves tickled me into action. I dressed quickly, climbed down to Reception and beat on the desk till Lola shuffled out from behind his curtain. His pyjama jacket hung outside his trousers and he was rubbing the sleep from his eyes.

'Get me a needle and thread.'

'What?' He looked like I'd asked him to fetch the bogeys. 'What for?'

I beckoned him close. 'I gotta problem. A bloke I know is going to get himself carved if he doesn't keep the customers happy. We'll want to sew him up, won't we?'

He stepped out of reach and sneered. 'You don't worry me, Mister.' But he went backstage and came back with a needle and a reel of blue cotton in one hand and the other outstretched. 'Twenty-five pee.'

I snatched it. 'Put it on the bill.'

He snarled. 'And tell your friends to stop away.'

I tripped on the stairs, thought better of it and went on up.

And who else?

I sat on the bed cutting the lining of my jacket just inside the lapel. I slipped the Armstrong passport down the inside and spent twenty minutes sewing the split. The Fraser papers I put in the bottom of the wardrobe drawer under my shirts, put my jacket on and left the hotel feeling lop-sided. Logan was sitting quietly in a white 3-litre Rover twenty yards from the hotel entrance. I stood on the steps and watched him while death tinkled up my backbone. Carson and his boys were boxing me in so tight I was suffocating.

There is a travel agent in Bloomsbury Way just west of the square. I left the Mini in Barter Street and walked round to the shop. It was hung with coloured posters and stuffed with pamphlets about holidays; birds in bikinis gave you the come-on to Split and Cossacks beckoned you to Omsk. I flipped blindly through the blurbs till the girl on the counter drenched me with smile. 'A night flight to Paris on the twenty-fifth please.'

She paged through a book and made a few notes. 'I'm sorry, sir. All Paris flights that night are booked.' She turned the page. 'I can get you a seat on the twenty-seventh.'

I shook my head. 'No thanks. Somewhere else.'

'I beg your pardon?'

I waved a hand at a poster. 'Brussels.'

She blinked. 'Yes, I can arrange a train from Brussels to Paris, but – '

'No. Just Brussels. On the twenty-fifth.'

'I see.' She didn't. 'What name please?'

'Fraser. David Fraser.'

She wrote out the ticket and I paid in cash. Logan was standing on the pavement opposite the Mini when I started up. I sighed and rubbed my eyes. Carson had closed all the gates except one.

Back in the hotel I put the air ticket in the drawer with the Fraser papers, rooted round the plug-hole of the basin down the passage and brought back a drop of something that had once been soap. I stuck a hair over the drawer with two specks of the stuff from the plug-hole and sat down for a think. I couldn't hold Carson forever while the axe poised over his neck. Anyway, the axe-man had one eye on me. The way I saw it, I had something Cain wanted and I was safe until he got it so I had to lose him while he played Get the Gelt.

I sat staring at the file Carson had given me for half an hour before reaching out like a man in a dream and starting to page through. It was like watching a horror film only there weren't any jokes. Carson's mark was a nutter. He'd been born in Bristol of Northern Irish parents and till he was seventeen thought Bogside was the bottom of the S-bend. About then this Frisby decided he needed a Cause and got his big chance in 1969 when half the population of Ulster was marching about in bowler hats while the rest chucked bombs and held countermarches. Frisby, aged nineteen, went to Ulster and joined the Provos as a soldier. He soon got a reputation as a nasty little sod and by 1971 was reckoned to be responsible for fifteen major bombs in Belfast plus maybe five assassinations. By 1972 he commanded his own unit, organizing casual sectarian killings on the streets.

The British had a clean-up in 1974 and nicked a few IRA activists, Frisby among them. He was held in Long Kesh and by all accounts the British gave him a nasty time of it. He was sprung after a month and nobody had fingered him since, but British interrogation methods must've taught him a trick or three because he next turned up as Divisional Intelligence Officer in Londonderry. Frisby's methods made bad reading for toddlers and it's enough to say that the Provos owed much of their recent success to information Frisby carried out of sound-proofed basements. He was promoted Chief of Intelligence in 1975 and still figures among the six most wanted men in Ulster. A bright lad, would go far. It seemed reasonable to stop him going further.

But Frisby had one point. I don't know what the British think they're doing over there either.

If you believed half of Carson's file most of the Micks in London were wandering the streets with sten-guns up their knickers. Frisby was reckoned to be here in an advisory capacity as well as to attend the trial mentioned by Carson, and the dossier ended with a list of names and photographs of those getting advice. There was even a picture of Frisby. Round young face with lizard eyes and a mouth like a razor-job. I dropped the file and had a think. Three of the listed names were reckoned to be Englishmen resident permanently in London, supporting the Cause for reasons known only to themselves. The most unusual name among the three was Hector Varsi. I put my jacket on and carried the file down to Reception. I had to wait my turn because Lola was busy booking in a mousey-haired brass hanging on the arm of a bloke smoking a cigar big as a drainpipe. Lola shut the book and they panted off upstairs leaving a smoke haze in the hall.

Lola leered at me. 'Help you?'

'Shouldn't think so, but try anyway. Get me the S to Z directory.'

He surprised me with his readiness. 'There you are. What name did you want?'

I stared at him till he backed off behind his curtain.

There were two Varsis in the book but only one Hector. His address was Steele's Road NW3. I scratched a mark under the name with my thumbnail for Lola and pushed the book across the desk. 'Thanks, sweetheart.'

Lola poked his head out. 'All right? Get what you wanted?'

'Sure. Now its your turn.' I picked up the file and stepped out into the street.

I got to King's Cross tube without noticing Logan but it wouldn't do to let him know I wanted him with me. The rush home was just starting and I joined the queue and bought myself a ticket for ten-pence, getting swept down the escalator like a pebble in a stream. It was suffocating down on the platform and I stayed back against the wall till the breeze from the approaching train rustled the litter on the floor, growing to hurricane force as the train crashed into the station and squealed to a stop. The doors opened and people fell out, sweating and struggling through the mob trying to get on. I wedged myself on the edge between the doors, got a grip on the partition next to the seats and pulled against the mass. They stumbled and swayed tighter, hot and aggravated. The doors closed and the train jerked out of the station, picking up speed with a steady hum while the wheels settled down to a regular rattle. I scanned the heads up and down the carriage. No sign. The train broke into Euston. I jumped for the platform as it stopped and carved a route through the mass of bodies towards the No Exit sign which leads to the southbound platform. The thing about choosing a No Exit passage at that hour is that the crowds are moving in the opposite direction to yours. It was like fight-ing an avalanche. I was forced close to the wall, fending them off with my arm. A tail would have been having the same problem but glancing over my shoulder, I couldn't spot any noticeable disturbance. I burst into the southbound platform as the train pulled in, vomiting people as the doors rumbled open. I stood in the nearest carriage entrance and turned to watch the exit. The heads jogged into the opening like bits of flotsam going down the rapids with the tide. Then the doors closed.

I stayed on the train till Bank, then changed to the Central Line and changed again at Tottenham Court Road. I got off at Chalk Farm feeling like a squeezed-out lemon.

Haverstock Hill is a relief after Euston Road, there being a few trees about and some variation in the buildings either side and it gets better the further north you walk. The motors were moving at a steady clip nose-to-tail and though odd people were leaving the station and staggering up the hill in ones and twos I couldn't see anyone I was bothered about. I turned left into Steele's Road opposite a pub called The Noble Art where Scotch had once introduced me to a pug who turned out quick as a twitch but a bit neddy in the noddy, which had put the frighteners on Scotch once and for all. Steele's Road is a leafy street that hides great red houses behind the twigs fronting the pavement. I walked slow as I dared down the pavement scanning each house in turn like a bloke that takes notice of his surroundings for the sake of it. Varsi's gaff was set back further than the rest, sporting a wild old garden growing through the paving-stones in front. The whole place needed doing up, which is no more than you'd expect from a middle-class revolutionary; he had to be middle-class living in a gaff like that. The front door was at the top of a flight of steps, massive-looking but not what you might call welcoming. All in all, anybody trying it on from the street had to be out of his mind.

I turned right at the end of the street and had a butchers along the sides of a couple of Victorian houses that blocked the view. That seemed the most likely spot so far. Barclays Bank stands on the corner of England's Lane and the houses on England's Lane back on to those in Steele's Road. Well, it's not exactly England's Lane because the houses on the south side are separated from the Lane by a line of trees and a narrow private road. They were big semis, older than the ones in Steele's Road. They must have had double-generous gardens because the distance between the private road and Steele's Road is at least a hundred yards. There was a narrow passage at the side of each semi leading to back gardens but, being a trendy manor, each and every one of them had a gate and a padlock to frighten off the villains. So far so good. I found myself on the corner of Haverstock Hill again. A few yards down was a pub so I dropped in for a quiet gin and a think.

If this was a normal B and E the best chance would've been through the houses on the private road and into Varsi's back garden. But it wasn't. If I was Varsi I'd have had a platoon spaced out in the garden and with Frisby to back me I'd have had the leg off the first bloke to put his size nines on the daffodils. If I was Logan I would have expected me to have figured a way by now, what with all that gelt in my pocket, and for the moment I was more worried about Logan than Varsi. I bought another mother's and went to stand in the cool by the door. Logan was staring into a newsagent's window across the street.

That was fine and I was glad he'd checked how well I was doing. The sight that turned the gin sour in my mouth was the man watching Logan a few yards down the hill.

Cain.

Eighteen

I stumbled across the gravel to a phone booth at the edge of the car park, tearing through the pages of the directory for Varsi's number. I could hardly find the holes in the dial. A bird answered, polite and well-spoken.

'I want to contact Frisby.' I had to try twice to get the words out.

There was a pause. 'Are you sure you have the correct number? This is – '

'I know what the number is. I want to talk to Frisby.'

Her voice was unworried. 'I'm afraid there's nobody here by that name.'

'Wait.' My hands shook as they gripped the earpiece. 'Tell him Carson is here in London.'

I thought she was going to put the phone down. Then: 'One moment please. I'll see if anybody here knows the name you mention.'

I sweated.

'Yes?'

'Frisby?'

'There is nobody called Frisby at this address.' The voice was deep and cool. 'Who is speaking please?'

I sighed loud and hard. 'Look. Tell Frisby I've got some information for him. It concerns a man called Carson.'

'But I don't know this Mr ... Frisby.'

'For Christ's sake!' I yelled. 'Where can I find him?'

'My friend,' the voice was smooth, 'you sound disturbed. Perhaps you should talk it over with someone who understands psychiatric problems ...'

'I don't bloody need understanding! Get Frisby!'

But the voice flowed on. 'Allow me to recommend a counsellor. Doctor Rattigan in Kentish Town is qualified to deal with your sort of aberration.' He hung up.

I stood with the receiver in my hand, sweat trickling down my wrist. I'd just made an appointment.

Kentish Town Road is a shoddy place lined by cheap chain stores and furniture salerooms hung with gaudy posters. You can walk from Camden Town to Highgate and not find a pub that'll draw your bitter in a thick glass. This Rattigan had a surgery sandwiched between a supermarket and a chemist's. The front window was obscure for half its height like a betting-shop, with a door at one end with one of those buzzing locks that let you in after you've said your piece. There were six or seven people in the waiting-room lining the walls like sides of beef waiting for the knife. The place was grim, all dark brown and cream, and the rat-bag behind the desk in the corner suited the air of misery. A table in the middle carried back numbers of *Weekend* and *Tit-Bits* but they didn't seem to be cheering up the patients, who were mostly getting on in years except for a kid that was squawking the roof down. Whenever the kid choked quiet one of the others would start coughing in a way that made you think he'd never make it to the surgery. The receptionist scanned me over her specs. 'Yes?'

I pointed at my belly. 'I've come about ...'

'Name?'

'Fraser. But ...'

She chopped through a card index. 'You are not registered with the doctor.'

'That's true. It's about ...'

'Have you your National Insurance number?'

I sniffed. 'No.'

'Then I'm afraid the doctor is far too busy to ...'

I gasped and bent nearly double. She stood uncertainly, glittering behind her specs. 'Wait a while. You had better sit down.'

I shuffled to a vacant chair and waited while the six of them were wheeled in, fed pills, and wheeled out looking worse. Finally Rattigan emerged rubbing his eyes. His coat was none too white. 'Next.' He looked at me as if he wished I'd disappear and let him get home. I walked to the door clutching Carson's file to my belly. The receptionist gave Rattigan a card and shut the door behind me. The surgery

107

was as bleak as the waiting-room – he didn't waste time or money on comfort. In one corner was the surgeon's couch, which looked like it could give you something nastier than what you came in with. On the far wall was an eye chart. Rattigan sat down behind a leather-topped desk surrounded by tubes and bottles of pills and bits of cotton wool. A sterilizing unit stood near the wall, decorated with lines of shining instruments. Rattigan began to scribble large jerky letters on a form and raised a hand without looking up. 'Sit down please.' He was a burly bloke in his mid-fifties. 'What seems to be the trouble?'

'It's about Frisby.'

The pen paused for a second while his left hand brought my card into his vision. 'Mister . . .' he glanced at the card, 'Fraser. Please describe your symptoms as concisely and lucidly as you can. I shall then attempt a diagnosis, and, assuming it to be within the scope of medical knowledge, a cure.' He still hadn't raised his eyes.

I pushed Carson's file across the leather top. 'Read it.'

He sat back in his chair and laid his specs on the file. His face was heavy and lined in planes that caught the light from the window. 'Mr Fraser. I run a busy practice. I am responsible for the health of two thousand people in this borough. I do not have time to indulge the fantasies of casual visitors.' He stood, pushing the chair back across the carpet. 'Will you please leave my surgery.'

I swept his specs off the file, snatched out the photograph of Frisby and slammed it on his blotter.

'Read it!'

The room was very still. Rattigan stood staring at the picture, breathing long and regular like a man in a deep sleep. He sat slowly, replaced his specs and began to page through the file. 'Where did you get this?'

'From a bloke called Carson.'

He closed the folder and turned to me. The planes under his cheek-bones looked like they'd been carved out of granite. 'What do you want?'

'Frisby.'

'Why?'

I tapped the file. 'Show him that and tell him Carson put it together. He'll want to see me.'

He rested his chin on his finger-tips. 'What makes you think I can help you?'

I stood up. 'Please yourself.'

'Wait.' He motioned me to sit. 'It may take some time to contact this Mr ... Frisby. Perhaps days. Where can I reach you?'

I raised a hand. 'Forget it. You haven't got days.'

'Where can I reach you?'

I wagged a finger. 'You can't. I'll call you tomorrow. If you haven't got Frisby by then the whole thing's buggered.' I stood and leaned on the desk. 'Give the file to Frisby. Tell him I can deliver Carson on a plate. He'll want to see me.' I left Rattigan hunched in his chair.

Two old-fashioned phone booths stand on the pavement outside the North-Western Poly on the corner of Prince of Wales Road. I parked the Mini round the corner and walked back. It was getting dark when I got into a booth and dialled a number.

'Harry old boy.' He sounded pleased. 'Where have you been?'

'Nowhere special, Major. Knocking about, trying to earn a crust.'

The Major gave his posh laugh. 'Snap. When shall we three meet again?'

'Soon, I should think.' I watched a couple of students nattering outside at the bus stop. 'Look, I've got a question to ask you.'

The Major purred. 'Fire away.'

'A mate of mine wants a shooter. Where can he get one?' The line clicked. 'Hullo? Major?'

His voice was soft. 'I'm here.' Silence. 'A gun, Harry? I hadn't considered firearms part of your stock-in-trade.'

'I told you,' I snapped, 'It's for a mate of mine.'

A bus swayed against the kerb and the two students got on. 'Yes,' said the Major, 'so you said.'

'Well?' I shifted position. 'Look. The shooter is for a certain party whose name I am not at liberty to reveal at this moment in time. OK?'

I heard him light a cigarette. 'Harry. It is now many years since I handled a firearm. Take my advice. Don't become embroiled in any action involving their use. It simply isn't worth it.'

I bellowed down the phone. 'I am not getting involved with any shooter! Do I have to keep on saying it? Now are you going to help me or not?'

He sighed. 'Very well. But you must understand that the information I give you may well be out of date. As I told you, I have had no dealings with hardware for fifteen years.'

'Fine,' I said. 'Where can my mate get one quick?'

There was a pause. 'Do you know Shelton Street?'

'Yeah.'

He gave me a number. 'Your friend will discover that the old boy there – if he is still alive – sells artists' materials in the ground floor shop. Paper, inks, pens and paints, articles of that sort. Tell your friend to be careful with his request. The old man does not suffer fools.' I heard him draw on his fag. 'Is your friend a fool, Harry?'

'Go on.'

'If the old man likes the look of your friend and his money – I say if – he will conduct him downstairs. In my day a great deal of his equipment was, well, army surplus. I'm told his stock is rather meagre these days. I assume your friend wants but one firearm?'

'Right.'

'Good. He doesn't cater for armies, d'you see?'

I held the door open with my foot. Traffic noise burst into the booth. 'Major, you've been a great help.'

His voice was bothered. 'I do hope so, Harry. Remember my advice, won't you?'

'I'll pass it on. See you.'

I'd parked the car and was walking towards the hotel when I thought I recognized a figure on the steps. Before I could be sure he'd gone. But the light from the entrance had shone briefly on his head.

Lank blond hair. By the time I entered the lobby I was shivering.

'Evening.' Lola popped out. He looked like he knew something I didn't. 'Warm again, eh?'

I gave him the baleful eye and walked on upstairs. I stopped outside my door, thinking of the figure on the steps, my hand twitching inches from the handle. I stepped clear of the opening, lay flat against the wall and threw open the door. It slammed against the plaster, shuddering in the frame as it bounced back half-closed. Silence. I put a hand round the woodwork and flicked the light switch. The room was empty.

But the hair across the wardrobe drawer was dislodged.

Nineteen

I phoned Rattigan from the reception desk while Lola tangled his turnip pretending to add a column of figures. It was eleven o'clock and by my reckoning Rattigan would be tied up in morning surgery.

'Well?'

He spoke slow and considered. 'Yes, Mr Fraser. I am told your Mr Frisby believes you may be of use to him.'

'So where is he?' I kept one eye on Lola; he was making a pig's ear of his arithmetic because he was listening to me.

'A pleasure boat leaves Camden Lock every day at one o'clock,' Rattigan murmured, 'travelling east. It's a pleasant day for a canal trip, don't you think?'

'Likes his audiences captive, does he?'

'I merely pass messages, Mr Fraser.'

I watched Lola. 'Sure. Camden Lock, one o'clock. The eastbound boat. I'll be there.' I hung up and turned to Lola. 'You may be a great lover, sweetie, but as a mathematician you're a fucking disaster.'

He hollered as I made for the stairs 'You owe me for four days.'

'See what I mean?' I peeled off three days' worth. 'Think about it. You oughta concentrate on what you're doing.'

Camden Lock has been trendied up in recent years and though the canal is the same the courtyard between the old stables has been done up with gravel and cobbles and white-painted bollards. All around are little craft shops flogging lumps of wood and string for twenty times their value and the first floor of the stables has been turned into a posh caff serving Nigels from NW1. When a place comes over

111

folksy as that you can bet that the first mob to be turned off will be the folk.

There's a bloke there that runs pleasure jaunts down the canal in an open boat; well, you can call them pleasure jaunts when they go west but going east the politest name for them would be interest jaunts because nobody calls backs of warehouses and rotten driftwood a pleasure except maybe the Nigels. The thing is that the old canals were useful before the railways because it was the fastest way of getting goods around the country. The tow-paths still skirt the water, some repaired for Sunday walkers but mostly still broken and weed-covered where gee-gees like steam engines used to drag several ton of barge, and I still remember the stories they used to tell me about the bargees. The trick was to move as fast as you could because the quicker you got there the better the boodle. Right? Just like these days. So you raced your gee-gees till they were blue in the face then swopped them for fresh at the next staging-point and so on and so on. Now it might happen that you were getting along so well that you caught up with the blokes ahead. Of course you'd be pissed off because you suddenly saw the prospect of losing bread through no fault of your own, which situation would not have fostered brotherly love for the berks in front, so when you got close you nipped off your barge and cut their tow-ropes. That was the idea, but you might well imagine that the berks up front had seen you coming and knew what to expect. Oh, you had to be mean to run a barge in those days because only the mean ones reached the other end.

The Grand Union Canal finishes at Ratcliff on the river which means if you start at Camden Lock you pass through St Pancras, Islington, Hoxton, Hackney and Limehouse. Now The Angel at Islington stands on a hill and the canal passes underneath. It's a long, long tunnel and in the old days they would unhitch the horses, lie on their backs on top of the barge and walk the barge through with their feet on the roof, which says something for the height of the tunnel.

I bought a ticket at the window under the arch to the courtyard and crunched across the gravel to the waterside. The boat was moored against the path, carrying a couple of families and a few ones and twos. There was room for a double bench on one side, a passage down the middle and a line of single seats opposite. The pilot stands on a platform about half-way along next to the engine which divides the boat into two, leaving a narrow connecting gangway. People were boarding at two points, the bows and the stern. I gave up my ticket, stepped carefully into the stern section and dusted off a double bench near the engine. It was a good choice. The motor was in front, blocking my view of the forward section, and by turning a little I could scan the seats behind me. My shirt was wet but that, I told myself, was because the day was hot. Which did not explain why my tongue stuck to the roof of my mouth.

Logan climbed in and sat in a single seat a few rows back. He was frowning in the light and his cheekbones glistened pink where their prominence had caught the sun. I watched him loosen his tie and shrug off his jacket, showing pale stringy arms as he rolled up his shirt sleeves. He folded out a copy of the *Telegraph* and measured the distance between us over the top of the newsprint. Four minutes. I saw nobody else I recognized. The pilot jumped in, a tanned bloke in a sweat-shirt and jeans doing his best to be matey with the passengers. I ignored him, wondering whether to walk round the engine casing and have a check towards the bows. At one sharp the motor spluttered, a pair of boys unhitched the ropes and the barge pulled into the middle of the canal. I glanced back irritably. Logan was reading his paper. We entered the lock a few yards down, leaving fumes hanging in the sunlight over the green of the water. The two lads ran along the towpath and wound the gates shut behind us. The boat settled lower and lower in the lock till the walls dripped on the passengers' heads, then the forward gates opened, the boys jumped aboard and we chugged under the road bridge towards the next lock.

The passengers were shifting about to get the best view. Most moved past the engine towards the forward section, leaving the stern empty except for Logan and me and a bird in denims and an Indian cotton blouse who came and sat right behind me as we nudged into the second lock. The lads got off and opened the gates.

The procedure was the same as before and there were at least twelve locks between us and the river. Through the gates the pilot steered into the centre of the waterway and the boat began to soak the tow-path with a bow wave as we picked up speed, forcing walkers off the path. It was like nosing between cliffs, warehouses and factories towering both sides so close at times that the sun never reached the water. The cliff faces were hung with gantries and lifting tackle, the steelwork sometimes closing across the canal to form a bridge way up between the cliffs. The brickwork at water level was slimy and broken, dotted with the mouths of old drains. Further down the sun sliced through a gap in the walls and we were running between houses with boats moored to private jetties; boats with names like *Scarlatti* and *Charlemagne II*. But canals are like that. One minute you're walled in by industry and the next you're staring into somebody's summerhouse. The bench shook and I turned fast. A man had sat beside me, pressing close. He leaned his elbow on the backrest and looked at me. Rattigan.

The slabs of muscle forming his face hung solemn as gravestones and his jaw was already shaded dark blue. He was wearing a green sports jacket and a check shirt open at the neck showing a mat of black hair cut straight at the start of his beard. Summer gear for doctors on the loose.

'Oh Mr Frisby, how you've aged.'

He gave no sign he'd heard but nodded at the bird in the seat behind. 'This is Marion.'

'I didn't think it was Frisby.' Marion's auburn hair tumbled about her face and shoulders, trailing over the slope of her tits so carefully wrapped in Indian cotton. 'How do, Marion. Don't get up for me.'

She inspected me like a dying moth. 'Get on with it, Geoffrey.'

I moved hard against the gunwale, feeling the passport dig into my ribs. Logan sat tense in his seat, paper folded on his knee.

The sun blinked as a tall figure edged past the engine cowling and moved down the passage towards the stern. Mister Cain paused, turned to face me, and settled into the seat behind Logan. I watched, ready to pray he'd got his priorities right.

He sat relaxed, one arm stretched along the rail, legs crossed, a hand in his lap. The breeze lifted a strand of hair on his forehead and he raised a palm to smooth it into place. It was some time before I managed to look at Rattigan. My mind was spinning and I tried to keep my speech slow. 'Did Frisby get the file?' He nodded, drumming his fingers on his knee. His hands were meaty and covered in coarse black hair. 'So where is he?' I glanced over Marion's shoulder again. 'Safe.'

'I'm glad.' My throat was drying fast. The boat rounded a bend and the tunnel came into sight. The bow wavered then steadied on the mouth where the edges were scored and the roof was polished by the scrape of boots. The tunnel was dead straight but I couldn't see light at the end. I scanned the tow-path quick but it was too far. The walls closed in, dripping, echoing till the engine noise shut against your mind

114

in darkness tighter than any brickwork.

Marion's hair brushed my face as she spoke close to my ear, and I was glad I was among friends, so to speak. 'Tell us about Carson. From the beginning.'

I couldn't see a thing. 'What,' I shouted 'do you wanna know?' The racket was deafening but Rattigan bellowed inches from my face, 'Where is he?'

Largo's eyes haunted the dark. 'In London like I said.'

'Where?' I caught a drop of Rattigan's spit on my face. Suppose he returned to his seat when it was still dark?

'That is information worth a lotta boodle to some people, namely you,' I hollered. It was no more than they'd expect and anyway if you don't try you don't win.

The girl rested a hand on my shoulder and I twitched like a cat. 'Listen Fraser,' she had bother pitching her contempt over the engine noise, 'trash like you ... raw material to Frisby ... pulp from which intelligence ... manufactured. Frisby is a successful intelligence officer ... ' did the dark stir? '... makes no difference ... you tell us now or Frisby later. But for you ... less inconvenient to speak now.'

I understood the last bit too well. 'So what'll you do?' I yelled. 'Chuck my fingernails to the fishes? You'll poison them.'

Rattigan's breath was hot on my cheek. 'Frisby needs to know where he might contact Carson.'

The noise filled my head like cotton-wool. 'I can't help Frisby till he helps me.'

'When will you next see Carson?' Was that Rattigan's jacket that brushed my sleeve?

'Pay-day.' Surely it should've been getting light by now?

Rattigan roared: 'Explain.'

'He ... asked me to do a job for him.' I shifted on the bench keeping my face to the stern.

'What?'

I cupped my hands round his ear. 'He asked me to do a job for him.'

'What sort of job?'

Surely ... light was beginning to reflect off the roof. I looked over the side. I could see the water-line against the brickwork.

'Look.' Strength flooded into my voice. 'Get one thing clear. I don't give a bugger about you and your private armies. I'm not involved, right? I'm not political.'

The noise didn't blanket the girl's sneer. 'Very wise. What . . . Carson ask you to do?'

The light tinted the planes of Rattigan's face. 'Oh this and that.' The noise was lessening. 'He gave me a file. I was to collect what information I could about the people in it.' I still couldn't see the stern.

'And?'

I focused on Rattigan. 'I came straight to you, didn't I?' Cain was too late to move now.

'Why?'

'Because . . .' the boat broke into the light and my eyes flicked shut. The sound of the engine spread into the air. I lowered my voice. 'Because I reckoned you'd pay for the information.' I looked back sadly. 'Now I've given it away.'

Logan was gone. Cain sat quite still in the same position staring at the water.

The girl seemed to be speaking. 'You're scum, Fraser. You know that? Oh, thank God there are some people on this earth still motivated by idealism.'

An empty seat. Was that what made my hands shake? People were waving from a canal-side pub. Rattigan gripped my arm. 'Fraser. You must arrange to meet Carson again.'

'I can't.'

'You will.'

I tried to concentrate. 'I can't without Frisby's help.'

Rattigan snorted. 'Mr Frisby tells me he is not accustomed to paying informers. In any case I would suggest that your role ended when you came to us. Very wise of you. However, you are now too deeply involved to do other than we ask.'

The boat was chugging between warehouses again, the engine strokes bouncing back off the cliff-faces. I could see Cain out of the corner of my eye. 'OK. If I turn Carson over to Frisby what guarantee do I get for my own safety?'

Rattigan straightened his legs. 'Absolute, provided you keep your word. The Republican movement is an honourable one.'

'You bet,' I said bitterly.

'Now,' said Rattigan, 'the meeting.'

I couldn't stop my eyes sliding towards the rear. 'I'll tell you something. Carson won't be alone, even if I do manage to call him out.'

'How many?'

'I don't know. At least one other. Tall fair bloke.'

'How soon can you arrange the meeting?' That was Marion.

'Soon as I get one more bit of gen from you.'

Rattigan narrowed his eyes. 'What?'

'The code-word.' I swallowed. 'The word you people are using when you call the press.'

'Why?'

'Take it from me. Carson isn't going to come without it.'

They looked at each other and Rattigan shrugged. 'Why not? Let me warn you, Fraser. The word is changed periodically. It will be useless the day after tomorrow.'

'Suits me. What is it?' Cain hadn't moved.

'Casement. Introduce yourself as Casement.'

The boat was approaching a lock near a bridge. I stood and eased past Rattigan's knees. 'This is where I leave you.'

'Fraser.' Rattigan caught my sleeve. I felt exposed standing there.

'Don't tell me,' I sighed. 'You'll know where to find me. If I try a double-cross your arms are longer than everyone else's etcetera.'

Rattigan had no sense of humour. 'We await your call.'

'Day after tomorrow, latest,' I promised. I stepped ashore as the boat entered the lock, measuring the distance between me and the bridge ahead, then skipped over the lock gates, jumped on to the tow-path and strode towards the bridge. My shoulder-blades were twitching until I set foot on the road.

I caught a bus back to Camden Town and picked up the Mini. The phone booths at King's Cross were all occupied except the dead ones and I waited a good ten minutes while some berk with a briefcase told his missus why he hadn't come home the night before. It sounded like he was losing. Anyway he left in a very aggravated state, catching his case in the door while I pushed past and started leafing through the S-Z for the number of the *Sun*.

'Get me the news desk. This is Casement.'

You could almost see the panic. There was a series of clicks then a voice tight with excitement said:

'News desk.'

'Casement. I will say this once. We know who killed Frisby. We know it was the English Special Branch. As a reprisal for this act of murder we intend to implement a bomb campaign. You will be advised. Warn your precious public.'

117

The voice stuttered. 'Can you repeat – '
I hung up and jotted down the number on the dial.

Down in the Gray's Inn Road *The Times'* public office was busy. I sat at a desk and filled in one of their smalls forms.

Boyne. Success. Await your

call 1100 hours 333 4782.

Cain.

I grinned at the girl behind the counter. 'No rush. Is the day after tomorrow OK? The twenty-third, right?'

She scanned a calendar. 'Correct sir. That will be fine.'

I left the building feeling like I had holes in my stomach. The day after tomorrow I might well be worrying about the holes in my head.

Twenty

Suddenly I was a celebrity without a name. All the papers carried the story on the front page but as you might expect the *Sun* hit the readers with a headline four inches high. The public was warned good and proper but what the press really wanted to know was who killed Frisby. The Army knew nothing about it and Scotland Yard couldn't confirm that Frisby had been the subject of any recent special investigation. In fact they reacted so strong that anyone reading the blurb couldn't help think there must be something in it. I had a giggle imagining the bother down at the Yard. The carpets must've been layered with bogeys that morning.

Shelton Street is lined with blackened Victorian warehouses and vegetable shops with open fronts being less than a spit from the market but among all that a good many tobacconists and other one-off stores make a fair living, to say nothing of the number of people who live there. The buildings are covered with clever-looking brickwork with rounded corners and there's enough wrought ironwork to rebuild the QE2 and still give change to the Japanese. It's a hassle getting through there in the morning on account of the lettuce leaves and dead tomatoes lying about as well as blokes pushing barrows. The Major's shop was half-way down. There was a bell on the door which tinkled as I entered. Inside it was an oasis of quiet smelling of paper and disinfectant. The floor was bare scrubbed boards and the customers were fenced off from the goods by a counter stained by two centuries of ink. Racks lined the walls at the back showing every known kind of ink, paint, pens and pile on pile of paper stretching to the ceiling.

119

A young bloke looked up. He was well turned out in a straight sort of way and his hair was very short.

'Good morning.'

'Morning.' I scanned the racks. 'I'm looking for something ... special.'

He stacked a ream of new paper on the end of the counter. 'Yes?'

I leaned on the counter. 'It's a bit hard to explain...' He waited 'Well, a mate of mine told me that you ... that if a customer comes to you wanting a certain very special item, you would be able to provide it.'

The boy raised his eyebrows. 'Yes?'

I frowned. 'Look ... is the old man here?'

He looked cautious. 'Who shall I say wants him?'

'Fraser. David Fraser.'

The lad opened a door between a pair of racks and shouted up the stairs. 'Dad?' I couldn't hear an answer. 'Mr Fraser to see you. What? No. He wants something special he says.' He left the door ajar and busied himself among the shelves. 'He'll be down in a tick.'

An old man looked round the door; he reminded me of a stone gnome come to life – pink rubbery face fringed by white hair.

'Mr Fraser?' He shuffled across the boards with worn-out shoes. He wore a striped shirt without a collar and a pair of National Health specs on the end of his nose. 'How can I help you?'

I cleared my throat. 'It's a bit complicated. I was just telling your lad that a friend of mine said that if a customer comes to you wanting something special you might be able to supply it.'

'I see.' His fingers were gnarled and wouldn't stay where they were put. He blinked like an owl.

'This friend said,' I went on, 'that even if a customer wanted something that wasn't to do with artists' materials you would do your best to help.'

The old man spoke over his shoulder. 'Colin.' The boy turned. 'Run and get me some cigarettes, there's a good boy.' He drew a few coins from his pocket with shaking fingers. The boy went out. The old man blinked over his specs. 'I may be able to help. I don't know. What was the name of your friend again?'

'Well, he's a major ...'

He chuckled. 'I've known more majors in my time than I care to remember. Some of them even genuine. What was your major's name?'

'Anderson,' I said, 'but you mightn't remember him.'

120

He fingered his mouth. 'Anderson? I don't think...'

'It would've been about fifteen years ago.'

'Anderson?' He looked up. 'Yes. Sandy hair, small moustache?'

'You got him.'

'Of course.' He winked. 'He was one of the not-so-genuine.'

'Sounds like him.'

He beamed, showing a fancy set of dentures. 'Good.' He beckoned me. 'You understand I am no longer as well connected as I was when I knew your major?' His smile stiffened. 'I rely upon a cash turnover. No credit.'

'Papa, you're speaking my language,' I told him.

He opened the counter flap for me. 'The boy knows nothing of this, you realize?'

I followed him to the door at the side. He clumped ahead down a narrow flight lit by a single bulb into a basement piled with boxes of paper. He shifted a few boxes and fiddled with a set of keys at a steel door at the back. 'Come in.' He locked the door behind us. The room was airless and hot. The smell of oil and steel was thick around me. Against a wall was a rack of twenty rifles and shotguns. And crates. Crates piled up the walls and forming an island in the middle. I whistled but he raised a hand. 'A meagre selection, I fear, but personally chosen. You'll find something here to suit your purpose.'

I picked the first rifle out of the rack. It was cold, oiled and wicked.

'The M16A1,' he nodded. 'American. They used it in Vietnam.' I balanced it in my right hand. It looked so fit it might go off. '5.56 millimetre. The magazine carries one hundred and twenty rounds fully loaded.'

'Christ.'

He scratched his nose. 'I hope I am not repeating facts you already know, Mr ... Fraser?'

I shook my head. 'You carry on.'

'Try it. Place it against your shoulder.' The rifle fitted snug. 'It weighs some seven and a half pounds loaded.' He frowned at me. 'Here. Hold it like this.' He showed me. 'Note the flash suppressor.' He pointed to the end of the barrel. 'Will you be using the weapon at night?'

'I don't know.'

He stroked the stock. 'Small calibre, but designed to produce a high velocity impact. Might I recommend a hollow-nosed bullet?' He paused

121

delicately. 'The marksman must needs be very experienced indeed if the hard-nosed variety is to tell.' He was watching me. 'The hollow-nosed bullet spreads on impact thus rendering the degree of accuracy immaterial. I take it your target will be . . . a living one?'

I scanned him. 'Right.' I put the rifle back in the rack, shaking my head. 'Too bulky. I gotta lot of carrying to do. It's too noticeable.' My eye fell on a case open on one of the crates. 'What's that?'

He lifted the case down like it was a baby. 'This, Mr Fraser is my current *pièce de résistance*. Not for you, I fear.'

The thing he raised into the light was a machine pistol, but such an item I had never seen before. The steel was engraved in flowery patterns, inlaid with gold and jewels, and the stock was of ivory carved fit for a museum. The old man held it in his right hand, caressing the barrel with his left. 'Made by Erich Boessler.' He could've said Khubla Khan as far as I was concerned. 'Commissioned by the head of a middle-eastern state. Herr Boessler worked on the engraving alone for three months.' He looked dreamy as he balanced the pistol in his hand. 'It came into my possession six weeks ago. Nine millimetre. Point 360 in English terms. Heavier than the old Lee Enfield at point 303.' He snapped awake and placed the pistol back in its case. 'I digress.' He pondered. 'Something portable. Have you considered a hand-gun?'

'Try me.'

He delved into a crate. 'Yes . . . this may fit the bill.'

The gun in his hand was almost hidden by his fingers. 'The Unique Model 51. Semi-automatic. It used to be known as the pocket pistol. Easily carried. Point 22.' I balanced it in my hand. It was like a toy.

'How many shots?'

'Eight. The magazine clips into the butt. Like this.' He withdrew the magazine and snapped it back into position.

'Point 22? High-velocity like the M16?'

'No no, Mr Fraser,' he chuckled. 'This little masterpiece is not designed for the same purpose.'

I shook my head. 'I've gotta have something with stopping power. And more accurate than a hand-gun. It might be a medium-range job.'

He put the Unique on one side, looking crafty. 'Ah. But there are hand-guns and hand-guns. Have a look at this.' He held up a tangle of leather webbing. 'A collector's item. The nine millimetre Luger.' The gun nestled snug in a holster attached to a system of belts and buckles. The holster was shiny and soft with use.

122

'How old is it?'

'World War One.'

'What?' I drew it from the holster.

He ignored me the way you ignore a bothersome kid. 'They manufactured two barrel lengths at that time. Eight inches and four inches.
This is the eight-inch model. Slightly heavy, but all the stopping power
you are likely to want with the right ammunition.' He held it at arm's
length in two hands and sighted against the cellar wall. 'The butt is
solid walnut.' The action snapped loud as he pulled the trigger. 'A
splendid piece, Mr Fraser. You can hardly do better.'

I was following the direction of his aim. 'What's that?'

A snakeskin case about two foot square stood on a box against the
wall. He lowered the Luger, picked up the case and brought it to me.
I set it on the floor and flipped the latches. The interior was lined
with scarlet velvet laid out in a pattern of slots and apertures, each
holding a component which shone in the light. He placed the open
case on a small table.

'This is the only model of its kind.' He watched my face. 'Manufactured on the continent by a specialist.' He selected a component.
'The action.' A block of steel machined into an L-shape with a circular
hole drilled through the base of the L. The length of the tail looked
hollow, fitted with a sprung breech and a slot underneath for the
magazine. The trigger mechanism was set behind the position of the
magazine, unguarded. The end of the action showed a pair of toothed
spring-clips. 'The barrel.' A tube no more than fourteen inches long
threaded at one end with a sight at the other. The old man screwed
the barrel into the action. 'Like this. You will hear a click as it drives
home. In that position the sight will be perfectly placed. So.' He
withdrew a frame of half-inch flat steel about two inches wide. It was
bent as an oblong a foot long, one side extending another eight inches
or so, turned down at the end to form a grip. 'The stock. Fits thus.'
He clipped the action block on the extended arm of the stock. Slots in
the arm coincided with the position of the magazine and the trigger,
and the rear of the action set firm against a flat upstand on top of the
frame. 'Bolt.' He slipped it into the rear of the action. 'Magazine.'

The whole was about two and a half feet long, spidery and lethal.
He balanced the thing somewhere near the grip. I stared. 'Ammunition?'

'9 mm. Hollow-nosed. I have several hundred rounds in stock.'

'I won't be needing much,' I muttered.

123

He put his head on one side. 'Seventy pounds.' I frowned at him. 'The only such model in existence, Mr Fraser.' He looked sly. 'I gather it fits the bill?'

'I'll take it. And a box of ammunition.'

He dismantled the spider, nodding as he set the components in the case.

I cleared my throat. 'How much for the ammunition?'

'Five pounds.' He snapped the latches shut and placed a cardboard box on one side. I counted out seventy-five pounds, picked up the case and shook hands.

'Thanks.'

He ushered me out and locked the door.

The boy was working in the shop. A packet of Players lay on the counter. The old man opened the shop door. 'Good luck, Mr Fraser. Give my respects to Major Anderson, won't you?'

I carried the case through the cabbage leaves to King Street. As I climbed into the Mini I told myself I might not have to use it.

Twenty-one

I took three bennies to see me through the night but it turned out I
didn't need them. I assembled the thing in the snakeskin case soon as
I got back to the hotel and spent the darkness sitting on a pillow facing
the door. By seven I was shaved and changed, dismantling the spider
and packing it in its box which I tucked away at the bottom of the
wardrobe. As soon as the shops were open I bought an 'Out of Order'
notice at a joke store on the Euston Road and paced across to King's
Cross station. My phone was occupied and I stopped just long enough
in passing to hang the notice on the door before getting a copy of
The Times from the bookstall. Then I settled down in the station
caff with a cup of tea. The ad was there alright.

At five to eleven I walked back to the phone booth with six cups of
tea swilling in my gut and it was probably that that made me feel bad.
I lifted the notice off and stepped inside. Carson was dead on time.

'Mr Cain?' I listened to him breathe. 'You appear to have done
well. Thank you.'

'Cut the thanks, Carson. Where's the money?'

A pause. 'The money is ready.'

'Where?'

'Mr Cain ...' my stomach lurched, 'I must express my concern
about recent ... events. The death of Mr Drake and two of my
colleagues.'

'All I want is the money,' I grated. 'The rest was your own fault.'

'Nevertheless,' he persisted, 'I must warn you I shall be adequately
protected when we meet.'

125

I sneered. 'Scared, Carson? Bring an army if you like. Only God help you if you haven't got the money with you.'

'As long as you understand.'

'The only language I understand comes in digits with noughts on the end. When and where?'

'Tonight. One o'clock. Park Lane garage.'

'I'll be there.'

I wiped my mouth with the back of my hand and dialled Crab's operator. 'Tell Crab I want him outside the Bayswater Road entrance to Park Lane garage tonight at one. One o'clock. Got that? Tell him I'll kill him if he's not there. What? No, just a private joke.'

I walked a little way down Pentonville Road and bought a pair of white cotton gloves at a secondhand shop. I wore them on the way back to the hotel.

Lola was paging through a copy of *Men Only*. He was missing a button on his shirt and hadn't shaved that morning. 'How do. You were up early.'

'I had to see a doctor.' I held up my hands. 'I've got a rash on my hands. Get me the phone.'

He stood back and pushed the phone through the dust with two fingers. I waited till he went behind his curtain. Rattigan sounded impatient.

'Well? I don't like your sort of interference, Fraser.'

I wiped my hand in long sweeps across the counter and traced the edge with gloved fingers. 'Stuff it.' My right hand worked over the phone. 'Listen. I'm seeing Carson at one tonight at the Park Lane Garage.'

'Mr Frisby will be there.'

'He better.' It wasn't every day Frisby took delivery of a package like I was wrapping. I hung up and whispered towards the curtain, 'Listen sweetheart. Just to show how much I like you I'm going to pay in advance up till I leave.' Lola appeared like magic. 'I'll be going on the twenty-fifth but I might not get the chance to see you.' I peeled off a few notes. It was awkward because of the gloves. 'And I was wrong about what I owed you. Here's the extra.'

'Going far?' He started to write out the receipt.

'Not far, no. A little place called Kano. Know it?' He shook his head. 'Cornwall. You should see it sometime.' I climbed the stairs and waited on the landing till I heard him pick up the phone.

Cain wasn't far away.

I can think of better ways of spending a day than dusting. When you think of the places you leave your dabs in the course of living and when you know the spite of the bogeys as well as me you don't leave anything to chance. I polished every bit of woodwork in the room, the doorhandles, the mirror, the wardrobe – even the walls. Then I checked through every stitch of clothing I had, cutting out laundry marks and brand-names. The labels I put in my pocket. The clothes went back in the drawer for good. At four I took out the snakeskin case. A couple of hours later I reckoned I knew the spider inside out. I could assemble and dismantle the whole works inside two and a half minutes. Then I lay down to wait.

I slept in a series of jumps for most of the evening, jerking awake every half-hour and reaching for my watch. Round eleven I got up and splashed cold water on my face in the bathroom, washing everything down and checking the surfaces before drawing on the gloves again. Back in the room I put my jacket on, felt for the passport, and loaded the spider's magazine before snapping the lid shut. A final wipe round. I stood in the middle of the room, sighed, picked up the case and left.

Lola wasn't at the desk downstairs but it wouldn't have mattered if he was. I let myself out the front door without leaving a thank-you note since I reckoned he'd been getting all the thanks he needed from one or two other interested parties. I drove down to Cumberland Place and spent half an hour checking through the Mini for anything that might point the finger my way. There wasn't much. Then I wiped down the leatherwork, the dash, the wheel and the handles. I left the keys in the car. With luck some tea-leaf would see his chance and by tomorrow the car could be somewhere like Frinton or Aberdeen. I set out on foot for Hyde Park.

The car park has an automatic gate that spews your ticket with the time printed on it. You give that to the attendant when you leave and he makes a charge based on the hours you've used. Nothing much happens during the night so round twelve he leaves his box and has a kip in a side room. Nobody can pass the barrier without hooting for him to collect. There are three escape stairs, all brick enclosures leading up to the pavement in Park Lane and the filter next to Bayswater Road. They're fitted with double fire doors that open out and panic bolts top and bottom. I slipped quietly into the staircase at the top of Park Lane.

The garage ceiling is about seven feet high lined by concrete beams in two directions and between the beams the strip-lights spray blue-white and leave no shadows. And below, the cars line up like a plantation of steel balloons. The floor was stained with oil and the whole place was quiet as King Tut's tomb. I walked close to the wall until I found the Bayswater Road exit.

The enclosure to the staircase takes up three car-spaces in the middle of the row. I tried the doors. The stair, narrow and dirty, started a few feet ahead. The strip-light nearest the stair had developed electric palsy, flicking in a rhythm that means it's about to bust, though I have known them go on for days like that. It threw an uncertain light round the stair which made it a good place to stay. I slipped down between two cars. The smaller one stopped short of the concrete wall at the back. I opened the snakeskin case and assembled the spider, clipping in the magazine last of all. Then I sat down.

The floor was cold against my arse but if I came out of this with no more than a bad case of piles I'd send Frisby an anonymous donation. I loosened my collar and wiped my face. Only two cars came in while I waited, both some distance away. The last one carried two blokes and a bird in evening gear, talking in loud English tones that said a lot for the booze they'd sunk. The bird was giggling like a budgie when they passed through the door to the main stair and the last I saw was a bloke's hand pressed into the pink satin of her bum. The door slammed, the echo died, and all returned to silence.

I was getting cramp and the flicker of the light was hurting my eyes. I looked at my watch. Ten to one. I stretched my legs and tried to massage my shins. The oil on the floor was staining my trousers and I couldn't sit still. About five to I heard a footstep. I flattened on the bonnet of a car and peered through the windscreen. A shadow moved along the rows of cars.

'Cain.'

Carson's was the sort of voice that carries but if I hadn't been expecting it I wouldn't have recognized the word. A figure emerged between two motors and crouched in the flicker of the strip-light. I eased the spider through my hands and stepped sideways between the staircase and the motor, the wall behind me.

'Here.'

128

The figure tensed. He was carrying a case. I moved towards the rear of the car, levelling the spider at his gut. He raised a hand to shield his eyes and stepped out.

'No further!'

He stopped. 'What the devil are you doing?' Carson sounded aggravated. He moved but I couldn't be sure what lies the light told. We faced each other across the roadspace.

'Put the case down.'

He wore a dark blue raincoat showing the white of his shirt collar at the top. 'Don't be paranoid, Cain,' he said it careful. 'Put that contraption down.'

The spider felt snug against my hip. 'Slide the case across. Easy!'

He bent and gave it a shove. In the twitching light it slid fitful like in a scene from an old-fashioned movie, stopping in the middle of the roadspace. I cussed him.

'Sorry.' He stepped forward.

'Leave it!' My bark echoed off the ceiling. I stood at the edge of the row scanning right and left. It was like a tube platform in the middle of the night. Not a movement. I stepped into the middle, keeping the spider in line with the buttons on his chest. I could feel the case with my toe.

'Key!'

He fumbled in his raincoat and chucked a pair of keys on the concrete beside the case. I scooped them in my left hand without shifting my gaze, felt for the latches and unlocked the case. Carson folded his arms and leaned against a car radiator.

'It's all there.'

I passed the spider to my left hand so I could feel inside the case. The gun wavered and if I'd had to let him have it then I'd have missed. The case was stuffed with bundles of notes. I drew out a wad and glanced down. Tens. Holding it in one hand I flipped my thumb along the edge.

'Bastard!'

The bundle was plain white paper sandwiched between two tens.

As Carson leapt for the space between two cars my trigger-finger twitched. The spider was pointing up and the bang deafened me. The strip-light shattered and broken glass showered over the motors.

Carson yelled: 'Now!'

The case leapt twice under the impact of a double smack. Standing square in the roadspace about twenty yards to my right stood two blokes, feet apart, wreathed in a tangle of smoke caught by the lights. I dived for cover and heard another explosion as bits of brickwork sprayed off the stair enclosure. Lying under the car, the spider pressed cold to my cheek, I could see their feet. They began to walk in my direction.

'Finish him!' Carson's voice again.

The feet separated into two pairs and began to move down each side of the roadspace.

Plop! The pair of feet nearest me stopped uncertainly. The left foot twisted on its side, bringing the bottom of the trousers in touch with the concrete. His knees hit the floor and a face drooped like an Arab praying until his cheek kissed the oil and the body slipped sideways, arm bent behind its back. The other's feet turned twice, grinding the heels into the oil. Plop-plop! The body crumpled against the radiator of a car and fell heavily on its back.

Silence. The smoke hung near the floor, clutching at my throat.

'Carson.'

I remembered that whisper. I could see Carson on his knees sheltering behind the cars ahead of me.

'Who are you?'

He was crawling towards the roadspace. A movement to the right caught my eye. Cain stepped slowly into the middle of the roadway. Soft shoes, knife-edged creases. Carson raised his head and measured the distance to the escape stair. Like a sprinter he poised on his fingers and toes, pointing towards the doors. It couldn't have been ten yards. He shot into the flickering light, head down, arms pumping.

Plop! The floor ahead of him puffed a cloud of concrete dust and the ricochet smacked into a car radiator. Water cascaded into the roadspace. Carson froze, arms high, legs wide like a man in free fall. Slowly his arms lowered to his sides and he turned to face the direction of the shots. Cain's feet stepped carefully over the body in the roadspace and came together about ten yards from Carson.

'Who are you?' Carson looked more puzzled than scared.

The voice was soft. 'My name is Cain.'

From the line of parked cars to the left, about fifty yards down, a white Jaguar broke loose in a wheel-spin, turned at right angles and roared down the aisle with headlamps blazing. Gun-fire and tyres screamed in concert. Carson leapt into the air, arms sawing, and crashed into a windscreen ten feet away. As I moved I saw Cain's feet stumble over the bodies in the aisle, then I was upright and running

130

for the doors, blinded by the blaze from the Jag and the cordite in the air. The lights blinked as a figure ran across them. I heard a voice yell 'There!'

The car park erupted in a thunder of guns and shattering glass. As I hit the escape doors a line of holes stitched a vertical pattern in the woodwork. I bust through a cloud of splinters into the stairway and took the stairs three at a time. Then I was gulping pure night air.

Crab was waiting a few yards from the exit, lights and engine off. He'd been half-asleep and came to like a thousand volts as I dived into the back.

'Move!'

He took off like a B52.

I cleaned myself up as we travelled. 'Got the case?' Crab was wide-eyed and driving like a madman. 'Yeah.'

'Tickets?'

'Yes.'

'And I'll be wanting my change.' I cussed. 'I didn't score as much as I'd hoped.' I thrust the spider against the glass. 'Ditch this after, will you?'

The late-night traffic closed behind us and Marble Arch swayed out of sight.

Twenty-two

If you've ever spent the night in the carsie at Heathrow you'll understand how I felt by the time I boarded the seven o'clock flight for
New York. But there wasn't even a bogey in sight, and passing
through the barrier with my case was no more difficult than crashing
the gates at Chelsea on a Saturday afternoon. By the time I settled
into my seat I was feeling quite perky.

TWA do a fair class of hostess. I'd been watching her since take-off,
her bum rippling under her skirt as she swayed up the aisle, the way
her hem lifted when she checked the luggage racks. She noticed me
after a bit. I got a smile as she passed and one time her thigh brushed
my hand as she stopped to chat with the woman across the aisle.
I ordered a Gilbey's but she talked me into a Martini which she
brought on my own special tray.

'Say, is this your first flight with us, sir?'

'Yeah,' I said, 'but if I'd known you were part of the deal I'd have
come before.'

She laughed. 'Is that right? We try to make your flight as comfortable as possible.'

'You do, love, you do.'

Things quietened down after a couple of hours and she stopped by
for a natter. Most of the others were kipping or watching Paul New-
man on the big screen. After all, it's a long way to New York.

'Comfortable, sir?'

I nodded 'How long d'you girls spend in New York, then?'

She showed a row of American teeth. 'Only a few hours usually, but this time I'll be spending a day there. Then I'm going home for two weeks vacation.'

Her jacket fitted a treat. 'Yeah? Where's home?'

'L.A.' She laughed. 'Los Angeles to you.'

My thoughts must've been showing. 'Well how about that? I'm catching a connection at New York through to L.A.'

'You are?' She flushed prettily.

'Hey.' I beckoned her close. 'Maybe you could spare enough time to show a lonely Limey round a few hot-spots?'

'Maybe.'

I sighed. 'Has anyone ever told you what a lovely smile you've got?'

'Many.' She gave me a secret pat on the hand. 'But I like it best from you.'

I settled in for a kip. L.A. was going to be good.

When I woke she brought a copy of the *Express*, her finger pressed against the address she'd scribbled in the margin. 'To occupy your thoughts.' She looked wicked and lovely. 'Second edition.' I savoured her scribble. She was called away and I sat grinning at the newsprint. I couldn't raise much interest in England any more, it seemed that far away, all strikes and bombs and trade-figures at an all-time low. Then I sighted the Stop Press column. The headline was fat: 'Gun Battle In Garage.' It was only a few words, a rough summing-up of what the Law and the press had found when they got there. The IRA was mentioned and the *Express* bitched on about carnage. One of the three bodies found had been identified as Leonard Carson.

Deputy Head Constable (Surveillance) Leonard Carson of the Royal Ulster Constabulary.

A sort of curtain cloaked my mind as I stumbled to the lavatory. Christ. Truly it is written he who stays one jump ahead gets the loser's boot up his arse.

Back in my seat I closed my eyes and tried to dream of Beverly Hills and Sunset Strip but something called me back uneasy and unwilling. I read the report again. Carson, his two heavies, and ... they meant

133

four bodies. The tingle down my back jerked me upright, eyes sweeping the heads of the passengers.

Of course they meant four bodies.
Or did they?

'Good luck Mister Cain.'